A Possible Fairytale

HADES

and the

Morning Star

Esther Tucker

Acknowledgements

For my children, because you are my heart. Each of you encouraging me in different ways. Each of you being your own, special light. For the angels, who have walked with me on my healing journey and have taught me the joy of living. For the fairies, who have taught me the meaning of friendship, balance and play, as well as respect. And finally, for my Hades, who will forever light my soul on fire, this book is written.

Foreword

There are stories that we remember that are so etched into our heart and souls that they become a part of our life. Beautiful, enduring stories, that at the end, you sigh. A sigh that is deep, indicating that your soul has been fed. We become a part of them as we journey through them with the characters. May you feel the timeless love as you walk through these pages. Such love that was born from the breath of the Creator Himself.

PART ONE

There was a time so long ago
that we have almost forgotten what once was known.
The origin, the beginning, of everything we see.
A starting point of journeys from where we came to be.
Whispered down the lineage from angels of all kind.
The story of the breath of life,
passed down through all this time.
It is noted, I was told, by an angel of good word,
That when we were created, a sigh was heard.
Not a sigh of despair, not a sigh of doubt.
But a deep sigh of love and commitment—
and it brought the world about.
For in that sigh was the breath of life,
So full of love and joy and some vigor to fight.
And out of that was born, as stardust shakes at morn:
Creation.

Out of the breath of life, occasionally, one soul would become two. In essence, they were one, gloriously complete soul in themselves, but together they had this dynamic that left an imprint on those around them. It is told by the angel Raphael that this is exactly what happened with two such angels.

In the beginning the Creator sighed, from that sigh a beautiful angel came forth, but just as it was about to finish taking form, it split into two. Two tall, magnificent beings. One was light, her wings as pure as the color of milk, eyes the color of dawns blue sky with hair the color of springs first daffodils. The other with wings as dark as coal, his eyes as dark to match but his soul as pure as hers. They were inseparable, balancing each other out in ways that only the other could supply as creation was being formed around them. The dark one was called Samiel while the light one was called Sara, this is their story, passed down through time.

We begin at the beginning of time, during this period angels were learning their roles as well as watching the many facets of creation from their places that they filled to keep creation, well, creating. Each one playing their part in the symphony that the creator had written in a score that shook the universe. Some angels are not so different than some humans when it comes to a thirst for power, so as the beings grew and evolved, so did their needs and what they felt they deserved for helping to create such wonders. It did not take them long to see in a world made of shifting energy, that energy was power, the more energy that they could absorb the more power that they gained. A simple but effective equation that started to propel some of them forward in what some groups considered negative ways.

Samiel was one of said angels. He was learning that by taking energy from other angels through competitions he soon could over power then next opponent without as much effort. The feeling that accompanied such victory was such a surge of energy and excitement he had to have more. He began to seek out such encounters, keeping much of it from Sara. She did not agree with said methods, Samiel had learned and he did not want to upset her. He often wished that he was more like her. She had such contentment and joy in watching as well as helping to create life all around them. She would show Samiel the leaves of a new plant with the excitement of a new bride at her wedding, pointing out the wonder of its intrinsic veins.

For Sara, Samiel felt nothing else but love. After all she was him and he was her. So he would listen, the joy on her face and light in her eyes becoming a reflection of happiness on his. Had it been any other angel Samiel would have brushed it off as too insignificant. Because Sara was a part of him he believed her to be the light side, he would never do anything to dim that light intentionally. For him, though, watching was not enough. Sara watched it all eagerly, the dawn of time. Each new day of creation bringing something new and exciting that they had not yet thought of the day before, she soaked in the newness and all of the possibilities.

Samiel had heard whispers from some of the other angels, whispers of dominating the creations that Creator was breathing into existence on a beautiful planet that had been carefully crafted by Creator. The angels had, a millennia or so ago, started to dominate each other, realizing what a good feel it was to take energy and power from each other. This created, well for a better term, angel factions. It started in small ways of robbing the other of their personal power and then would sometimes erupt into war between the different factors.

Sara would drag Samiel out of the skirmishes, for this he was often unappreciative. "How will we ever get ahead without more energy? We must have more power to be, Sara."

In which Sara would reply, "We are being, we are helping to create. Draining others of their energy, through fighting or any other means, only drains yourself first Samiel. Take the energy you already have and invest it into creation around you. Into your own being."

On many levels Samiel knew her to be right. After all, how many times had it taken him days to replenish his own energy after a skirmish, even with Sara taking such good care of him. It was the days that he won, could over power the next angel, that kept feeding his hunger for more.

"Creating brings a feeling of power as well," Sara said.

Yes, but it wasn't as instant as just taking power, therefor to Samiel it just wasn't as satisfying.

He had one especially draining encounter. The angel that he had fought had a much higher vibration that he had himself, easily overpowering him. Perhaps Sara was right. He went with her the next day, she was going to Earth. That was what they had agreed on for a name for said planet of greenery and beauty. They played by a spring that was so blue, it's small waves beating against pebbles, creating a vibrational purr in the air. They played with the new flora and fauna—fascinated with the humans.

In that early time of being, man and angel walked and talked together, speaking freely. Learning and growing from each others strengths and weaknesses. Through these conversations Samiel realized that the humans had abilities that the angels did not. It seemed to him that they had more power. Why would Creator allow that? They could feel, smell, taste. Love with the entirety of their being. Samiel watched as they took dominion over the plants and animals in earth.

"We should have done that!" he lamented to Sara.

"We would not be free to fly and play, to help create in the capacity that we do," she replied. Her blue eyes were on fire with the sunset before them.

Every day Sara drug Samiel to watch the sun set and rise. Secretly he was also in awe while the colors painted the sky, but he had to fuss so Sara felt like she was special that he went. She would hum a song that was not a song. It was more of a vibration of what that moment felt to her. It carried the vibration of love, wonder, and joy. While she hummed she would glow, like a nebulae in its glorious prime. Samiel especially loved her hum. It would settle his furrowed brow as he pondered the ways of power, questioning the creators logic.

One such sunset Samiel was following Sara through a garden, creation circling their beds for the night. There was no need for light as Sara was still humming, her glow softly lighting the dark around them. They came upon a camp full of humans, laughing and singing songs that they were obviously making up as they went. Samiel's brow furrowed as he tried to make out all of the words that he was hearing. They were telling tales in their songs, while passing around a liquid that made the songs, and tales louder. He wondered what that liquid was as it also seemed to make them happier with every swallow.

Off to the left were a couple, clearly only intent on each others presence. Sara felt their joy, smiling with them. Samiel felt resentment. He had often coveted the humans perception of taste, sound, smell, hearing, and the more difficult one to watch, touch. He knew they took it for granted and that thought always angered him.

"They have no idea what they have Sara," he lamented. "I see them reach for each other, all the while taking it for granted that they can feel the others skin. I want to have that type of power, the power of sensation. That is something that we should have been gifted with as well."

Sara took his hand. "I feel you," she looked in his eyes, her joy lighting hers, "and what I feel when I feel you is a great love and contentment. A feeling of belonging and home. I feel so much when we are close to each other."

Samiel shrugged her off. "Yes, of course I feel deeply for you, but we do not have the physical means of expression as the humans do. Don't you want to know what a kiss feels like? Or the reddest of wines when it touches your tongue, does it burn as they say? The joy on their faces as they smell what the older ones cook, even the repulsion of what they call stench. How can we experience everything of we have not experienced humanity yet?"

He left her there, to ponder the words that were spoken, those words would trouble her for many days to come. Those words of foreboding echoing the truth that was nagging in her mind. Her world was full, so full of wonder and joy. Of being and shining, of sharing a glow that existence had granted her and part of that heart beat, that luminescent glow, was her great love for Samiel. When they were not physically together, she could still feel him. She had tried to show him through her eyes all the beauty around him. Especially in healing and helping humans, answering their prayers and guiding them down beautiful paths when they asked. After that conversation, she knew, Samiel had made up his mind and she could feel it in the pit of her stomach, Samiel would choose to fall.

Samiel had brought this up a few other times, how long ago was difficult for Sara to say as time is different for angels than it is for us, not being linear, but just being. From what she understood through his words of explanation, certain angels had felt creator did not do for them as he had done for humans. After all, look at the power they had, not just over the animals, but each other. A little blunt force and you could own anything. It was much more difficult for angels to take power from other angels. They did not just give it away as the humans did. Through happenstance, Angels had found out they had the choice to "fall", as they named what was simply coming to earth and living amongst the humans.

When they first started doing this they still had certain abilities and gifts. So much so that the humans worshipped them as gods amongst them. The humans believing this to be infallible evidence that they had come from the heavens, so they must be gods. What they did not understand, they became afraid of and began to worship, giving their power away so easily. Samiel had watched the very first few that had fallen. He felt that these gifts and abilities would not always be so easy to keep as time evolved. It was now or never. So enthused was he as he pondered the totality of what those fallen angels now possessed, especially over those that he felt ignorant, less than what his superiority would ever let him be.

"Don't you see Sara? That is truly our purpose, power and dominion." He had found her in a garden, healing a wounded bunny.

She would be his captive audience while she did it, he smiled. Looking up she smiled and then sighed, "Samiel, I am making a difference here, right now, healing."

Samiel replied, "Yes, but that creature does not have the abilities that the humans do, it does not need to be guided, it simply knows. Humans need guidance, they need true leaders that they can look up to that possess innate intelligence."

"Oh Samiel, you are happy with me, especially as we play, why ruin all of this over more power, isn't joy a power in itself?"

Samiel did not look up, dark eyes piercing into the ground. "There is no joy without power." He walked away without making eye contact.

With that discussion came the knowledge to Sara that her beloved Samiel would not stay with her if she could not show him that joy was a power in it's own. She took special pains after that conversation to show him life through her eyes. She felt it may be more of a memoir of remembrance at this point, but she was not going to just "roll over" as she had heard the humans say. They did seem to give their power away often. She feared the alternative to not giving up, and used her love and connection to him with it's raw force to keep him close to her just a little longer.

Those days that followed were magnificent to Sara. They helped with the formation of new waterfalls as well as the creation of new flora and fauna. Sara would get so excited over this, her ideas rolling off her tongue faster than she could speak. They marveled at the play of creation, and they played along with it, dancing with the fairies at the sunsets, joining in the worship at the sunrise.

"I think if I ever did fall, I would not want to be a human, I would want to be a fairy! They call to me, with their light and laughter and care of the planet around them," Sara said after a lovely dance. Samiel agreed that Sara would, indeed, make a most lovely fairy. Adding that he believed she would have rainbow wings. "Maybe no wings, I feel that they are cheating here and there a bit with them. Perhaps just the light in me would be enough to carry me Samiel."

Samiel was once again moved by Sara's keen awareness of what she did and did not want. He was still trying to figure the totality of that question in his mind. He only knew for certain that he wanted more power! He needed more than just wind in his wings, and unfortunately, more than just the love of Sara. He did not realize the power that they had with their connection. He could only see raw power, such as what the humans in front of him had. He once again felt that stabbing pain of resentment, that this should have been for angels. Such power of sensation, the ability to feel so much.

9

Thought Samiel to himself: "I would know what I had, I would use it to all of its capabilities with all the magnificence that it carries." Those words that he spoke that day, so close to the beginning of time, echoed through his lifetimes, they were part of his becoming.

So, the day it came it was not the shock it could have been to Sara. Samiel held her face in his hands, while words rushed out of his mouth of the epiphanies that he felt his soul had given to the rest of his angelic existence. It was a truth he simply knew, he had to fall. He had to finish becoming and he could not in this one place of existence. He needed the power that came with such a transformation, and though Sara was a part of him... well sometimes we have to leave a piece of ourselves in order to find the whole of our self.

Samiel had not really preplanned the day that he did it, he simply knew it was time, time for the next phase of his being. Destiny was ruffling his black feathers that he sported so proudly. He once again put a hand on each side of Sara's face, she liked that human gesture, telling her it was time.

"It's time for me to fall and find my place in the new world, I want you to come with me, I want you by my side, will you come with me Sara?" Sara's heart clenched, his words tore into her very existence. What response should she have to such a quarry?

She loved him greatly, he was her outside of her, his existence lighting her fire. No matter the transgression or the darkness they had faced, they had faced it together, knowing it would be that way until the end of time and space. Sara had often thanked Creator for this connection and love. It was difficult to explain to any one that had not experienced such a connection, being one breath, spoken into two, there were no two, only you. She had known that this day was coming, that she would have to find the courage to be as true to herself inside as she was outside.

His eyes were so imploring, though. Begging from their soul. "Come on Sara, let's go on the greatest adventure of our life, experiencing the world through sensations we cannot have as angels. I love you, come with me." Her breath caught, never had he spoken out loud what they both knew existed. It was his interactions with humans through the years that had taught him the words, but he knew the meaning the moment he was created. To hear him say it, Sara began to vibrate and glow, humming without meaning to. The light in her eyes would not easily dim as she held those words in a place that would only ever be for Samiel in her heart. But once again she knew, she was her own entity, and as much as she loved him , he would be taking all of her being to a life that she was not ready for, possibly not even meant for

"Samiel, I can not go with you. I would dim my light for a weak power that the humans call sensation. As a human I don't know that I would make the difference that I make now. Most of them are confused as to what they are supposed to be doing, I know my purpose and being in angel form serves that purpose the best." And for the first time in their existence, she could not meet his eye, she knew that she would falter if she did. She would abandon her purpose to follow her heart. She had seen the outcome of that before, it never ended well.

Samiel had a wounded look of shock on his face. He never dreamt that Sara would not follow him. They had always been together, since that first breath. She looked up and met his gaze, in that moment he faltered, but he knew that no matter how much he loved her, how much she seemed like him outside of him, he had to go on this journey. He had to experience what he had watched so earnestly. He did not want to be human, per say. There was no glory in that, he wanted to be worshipped, the best of both worlds. With Sara's words he let go of her face as he took one, deep, knowing breath. He felt, he knew, inside of himself, that she would come looking for him, that she would come home. That was the last time that Sara ever saw Samiel in an angel form.

Samiel fell shortly after that discussion. Sara went on with what she felt was only existence. Angels do not feel at the depths that humans do, Sara was grateful for this in the days that followed. She could not imagine this feeling amplified. She felt only half there. Ever since she was created she could "feel" Samiel. Reach with her energy, and feel him, no matter where he was. This had been a comfort she did not even know that she had, until it was gone. She repeatedly would pause throughout the following days and feel for him, the other part of her soul and heart. In that pause all she felt was an echo of where he once was. She threw herself into her creations, more lovely flora and fauna, that had always calmed her in the past. The feel of creating, coursing through her being. But there was no Samiel at the end of the day, to hear of her adventures and marvel with her at the joy of being. No Samiel at day break to watch the splendor of the sunset and worship with all of creation in that moment. No Samiel.

She was keeping one eye on him after the fall, not her eye of course, she could no longer feel him, for when he fell, he fell hard. Her Samiel had become a god to the humans, a god that they worshipped and feared, a god that guarded the underworld. Sara felt that this hurt her the most.

She was light, love made her physically glow. She loved creating and helping that creation flow, the thought of her beloved Samiel punishing lost souls, that was atrocious. Definitely not adding to creation. She remembered his excitement when they had first created things together. She could not imagine how he could be so different now. Perhaps being away from her had done this to him? And with that thought it was not even a wing span of time before she decided that she should fall as well.

She would find him. She wished that she would have asked him more questions or paid better attention when he had talked of falling. Now she had a list of questions. How do you land where you want to? How do you know where you want to land? She did remember him saying that energy follows intention.

Set your intention and your energy will follow. With her lonely, grieving heart, she set her intention towards Samiel, that heart loved him so much, it so wanted to be a beacon and a light for him. That was her last thought as she fell. She closed her eyes and awoke as a glorious being of light and energy, brighter than she had been before. Her desire to help guide the lost was so strong as she fell, that she awoke as the morning star, caught in the night sky between who she was and who she would be, while leading the lost home.

PART TWO

In the chatter of the birdsong.

In the softness of the dew.

In the silence of my breaths...

I love you.

In the fire of the sunrise, as day climbs to mastery.

In the dance of the lightning bugs, that's where you will always be.

When Paris nights were plenty, one just burst into song.

As notes flowed from the heart, nights were never long.

That's where you'll be.

Tucked between yesterday, almost in the now.

I'll feel the echoes of your touch, I'll forget the why and how.

And just beyond morning, the second star to the right,

I'll hold you for eternity, we'll live our endless night.

When Samiel fell he set his intention for what he felt was the best chance to give himself in increasing the likelihood for more power. He had been watching the humans for such a very long time that he felt fairly confident in his choice. He had noticed their tendency to give their power away. Freely. They just gave it away.

Of course, not all of them were like this, causing some wars and battles here and there, but, for the majority of them they just followed the leader. Such innate power in the numbers willing to be followers. Samiel felt then, that taking a place of authority should be fairly simple.

Other angels, as previously mentioned, had been doing this for a length of time. Controlling how they fell, they would use their angel powers to take a humanlike form. Some of them missing the mark a bit. That's where some centaurs and such have originated.

They were more beautiful, taller and stronger than humans, whether they fell as a male or a female. One of the first to fall did a miracle, well, really by accident, the humans were so impressed that were near, they named him a god and began to worship. His name was Zeus, and he quickly over powered those that came with, and, after him.

Samiel had been a very active player in the beginning of time when the angels first recognized that they could take power from each other. He felt that same energy as "the gods" on earth fought each other to be the mightiest, using humans as pawns this time. Samiel felt that was especially brilliant, seeing how the humans were eager to give it away. And he was going to be part of it.

So intent was his desire, so born of raw passion, that when Samiel fell he became what history knew as Hades, god of the underworld, master of dead souls. This did not happen the moment his feet landed on the earth. His lust for power was taxed in the atrocities that he committed to own that throne. His soul never

17

completely Samiel again. He had done things that were questionable even to the other gods, so much so that he had lost his sense of where he came from.

It is always important to remember where you came from. Often those moments of remembrance lead us to where we are and where we are going. In remembering, with gratitude, the obstacles that we have overcome, we use that strength and power in the present moment to create the reality that we want, with a vibration to match. We use our internal magic.

Samiel, who we will now call Hades, had so lost his beginning, that his moments of unbecoming were at times more than the steady flow of becoming. That flow that nudges us through as we push forward and gain clarity that is needed to further our joy through our purpose. Hades had attained the power he had lusted for so long, but in the evenings, especially in the quiet, he felt the missing pieces. He tried very hard to keep it from being that quiet, because he had a very hard time grappling with the reality. He did what we all do, he tried to remember the beginning, how did he end up this way, without really remembering.

Many millennia had passed when he once again felt like he was missing something, but something on the outside of him, something good. So many atrocities that he had committed to get to his place of power, even he felt there was not much good left on the inside of him. He had to do it of course, all of it, to get to where he was. But he sat and remembered that day, he reached back in his memory behind the horrors, and he remembered Sara.

Bright, beautiful, Sara. How dark it suddenly felt in his kingdom. So much loneliness went into the creation of his empire. He had, though, felt, tasted and conquered what ever he desired on his way through his pilgrimage of power.

He had not found anything, though, that made him feel like Sara did. That warm comfort, that spark in his chest, that knowing that her simply being, that she was. Yes! That is what he needed! Sara!

His faced clouded, rumblings echoing throughout the underworld. How would he reach Sara? How would he get a messenger to her? She was dimensions away from him. He was unsure of how much time had passed since he had seen her.

He spent several sullen days before he decided to try to forget again. This was something he had learned from the humans, the coping mechanisms of forgetting. He could not miss her if he did not remember her in the moment. He clapped his hands while doing a small shuffle dance to the left, thinking that was the best thought that he had in a decade. Satisfaction lit his dark eyes as he called on his staff.

His staff were the poor angel souls, many of whom had fallen with him, that just did not make it in the quest for godhood as he had. They were obviously superior to humans, especially in strength and longevity. At least he could give them a purpose, he, Hades was god of the underworld, but his servants still had dominion over the human souls that lived there, chained in their own fear and guilt.

Hades often marveled at how many human souls stayed in the underworld, their belief in their "bad" so strong that they kept themselves in the darkness, bound, while swearing they never wanted to be their. So afraid and guilt ridden they made the underworld not only possible, but a flourishing economical oasis for the mighty Hades.

He had watched in wonder at the beginning of time, the look of pleasure on a human beings face for the things that they tasted or felt. They could physically feel the grass on their toes, and they really seemed to enjoy this. Once, before his fall, he had stumbled across a man making love to a woman. He saw the look of joy on their face as they experienced the physical moment of ecstasy together, felt the glow their soul emitted as they embraced the moment. He had wondered what that would feel like with Sara, such intimacy as that. And once again he marveled at all they had and how they so easily gave that away.

These human souls had made it possible for him to live a physical existence with their innate desire to worship, to believe in anything other than themselves. Hades had often thought how formidable as a creation each one would be individually if they ever put the energy of belief into themselves that they put into every thing else.

They had given him the amount of power he needed to have what they had, their senses. He had felt, tasted, smelled and heard an incredible amount of things since he had fallen. So many of them magnificent, just as many horrendous. All of them an adventure. But without Sara.

Not thinking of her was becoming increasingly more difficult. His servants were hosting mighty events of valor as well as the arts to keep his mind occupied, and his hands, to little avail. This was surprising as Hades was especially fond of sporting human against human in any fashion and see who wins.

The gods would then sport their champions against each other. The faith that these human beings put into them gave them the power that they needed to be the gods that those same humans wanted them to be. Even though said gods used them for pleasure and sport, adding to the power struggle they continually played upon. The humans had so little faith in themselves with an innate belief that they had to be led by someone bigger than themselves, they made it easy. In fact, their entire belief system had provided Hades his now lavish existence.

He of course had no baseline before his fall, but from the bite of a sour apple to the taste of a beautiful set of lips, those sensations from tiny taste buds were nothing short of miracles. Then there was touch, something that he would not have known how to fantasize about before he fell. He would not have been able to imagine the amount of joy and comfort that it brought with it. The feel of soft fur, the warmth of fire, but no too much. Here his mind gravitated back to Sara where he began to brood again.

He did not have friends in his current role, becoming the king of the underworld did not win him the admiration of love, only fear. There was an abundance of that resource that he had tapped into. He did have servants, as previously mentioned, and they realized these mood shifts were affecting their reality. His man in charge had been his friend before they fell together, not only his but Sara's as well. His name was Osephus and he had been with Hades for long enough to feel even a subtle shift in his vibration of feeling. It had taken many years for Osephus to gather that the current mood was brought by thoughts of Sara.

Osephus realized that Hades himself did not realize what these thoughts did to his being, mostly because he was a narcissist, in part because he lost the need for anyone else. He believed his grandeur to be enough totality of being, so much so that he did not recognize the emotion of missing someone, becoming more intolerable in those moments. Osephus pondered these thoughts as Hades was stomping around the underworld and no one was doing anything correctly. Osephus had not learned yet in that lifetime that many times other peoples behavior has nothing to do with us but everything to do with them. Once we stop taking it all so personally new life begins to unfold. Even in the underworld.

Osephus pondered the matter at hand and felt relief when an answer seemed to come to him. He remembered Sara and her effect on the master, that's what Hades needed, he felt, companionship.

True companionship though, not the entourage that would come and go at all hours. Hades needed an equal. Perhaps he, Osephus, could find Hades another Sara. Here I must stop you dear reader and kindly state that perhaps Osephus was in this role for a reason as he truly was not a leader, he was very much a follower especially in his lack of thorough thinking and thought processes.

He spent several days assessing women in the underworld when it struck him that if Hades needed an equal it probably should be a goddess. This would be more difficult than what he had originally felt. Osephus tapped the chair beside him, watching Hades pace, trying to think and watch at the same time. He felt Hades had helped in grow in this area as prior to the fall it had been watch or think, never the necessity for both.

He stood a little taller as he thought of the growth and progress that he was making. He had learned through painful repetition that one really did have to do both, watch and learn to survive. Evolution when paired with survival makes an excellent bed fellow. Osephus was relieved when Hades announced he would be at the great hall in the afternoon as then he could go back to simply thinking. This is where he felt he would finally make the most progress in the growing dilemma.

That afternoon he made a list of the goddesses, there were more than he realized, that was a bit of a relief. He had asked other staff for all the goddess names that they knew as well, one of the cooks when finishing their list asked a valid question, what did Osephus think he could do to "catch" a goddess. Osephus paused his writing.

Servants did not speak to gods that they did not serve. You were spoken to when near them. He sighed deeply with this new problem. Osephus had been a cherub as an angel, he faintly remembered that life, the joy and freedom it held, in moments such as this.

He had lost both of those when he fell, believing the other angels and their tales of power and glory. He had rose to a level of power with Hades that others did not have, but he did not have what it took to be a god. They had committed acts in their climb to power that would take some lifetimes to erase that karma.

The cook was right though, he could not walk up to a goddess and talk to her. Not only for the previously stated reason, but if Hades found out he would assume that Osephus was "god hopping", looking for a better fit per say, and he would destroy Osephus. Best to avoid that he thought.

Osephus thought for a brief moment that perhaps he could just tell Hades the truth, but he knew Hades had long ago given up kindness, to the point he would not perceive this for what it was, kindness. Osephus shuffled in his thoughts, of course it was self preservation as well, more of something to ease the rest of their lives.

It was at this point that he realized he would need to find someone smarter than himself to help find a solution to this pressing dilemma. Who did he know with such expertise? He tapped his forehead, he found this helpful when thinking, he had seen it on a human statue and had adopted the practice since. It seemed to bring the underlying thoughts to the surface more readily, and in that moment it worked! The Oracle came to mind. Of course! The Oracle! Why had he not thought of her sooner? She was Hades seer, using different manners of divination to talk to the universe for guidance that Hades needed help with.

Osephus sprinted off to find her, well, it was more of a lively shuffle. At one time Osephus had been a truly beautiful angel with magnificent wings. His demeanor would droop when he remembered how he had looked. The memory was fainter now after centuries.

The fight and lust for power along side Hades had changed his physical appearance as well as his soul. He was short, somewhat shriveled, with small black eyes that would some times get lost in staring at you. He walked with a limp as he had a gimp leg, no one could recall what made it that way though. What was seared into his memory and added to the acid in his stomach was the memory of Hades being Samiel, and as his friend coaxing him to fall. Osephus remembered the lively conversations and excitement of what they were going to do together.

Osephus believed that originally Hades did believe all that he was telling himself and Osephus was the truth. But as Hades grew in power and notoriety he started to use Osephus as a stepping stone and less of a friend. When you are treated like you are less than, especially by a friend, day in and day out, you begin to believe that you are less than every one else.

Osephus had not learned how important it was to keep positive people in your inner circle, so he began to feel and believe what he was hearing. Once a proud, beautiful angel, vibrating with the glory of life. Now a shrunken, gnome like creature that could no longer stand the sight of his own existence.

Sometimes he wondered how he would be now if he would have stayed that beautiful cherub, he shook off the train of thought, no sense dwelling on it, it was what it was now. He shivered as he quickened his pace, the underworld had what he like to call "misery currents", blasts of hot or cold humid air that would engulf you, feel like a short stent of strangulation, and then it would move on. Hades interior decorator had out done himself on that idea. The most recent one bringing his mind back to the task at hand, he was eager to get this process started.

The Oracle had a dwelling, almost hidden in the underworld as it was cloaked accordingly to keep herself from prying eyes and those that would use her. She was already at Hades command, she would not repeat that mistake with another power hungry god. The gods liked to visit each other while making it a sport of collecting what the other one had that they themselves did not have. The fact that some said possessions were alive and breathing did not deter any of them in the least.

In the beginning she had been Zeus's oracle. The memory of Hades taking her was not a pleasant one, he was very pleased with his spoils. The gods had lost their ability to talk to the sprit world for guidance, this they coveted greatly, making an Oracle one of the most valuable possession's that a god could own. She had thought of fleeing, but there was really no where for her to hide from them as they were so spread out, one would just find her again and she had vowed that would not be a reoccurring theme.

Honestly, of the gods she had been with, Hades was the milder, so if the fates decreed she would be an oracle, she would stay his by her choice. With this in mind she had made it no easy task to find her in the underworld. She had created an illusion around her cottage to help keep her cloaked from those she did not want to find her.

If you looked directly at her dwelling, you could not find it. It could only be seen by gazing from the very corner of your eye. Either eye would do, but it had to be that farthest corner.

The Oracle had explained to Osephus, after he remarked on how genius that was, that often we disregard those things that are seen just outside the corners of our being, choosing to not add them to our reality, no matter how very real they are. Easily then shaken off and forgotten.

If only humanity knew all that lived in the corner of their vision, that peripheral domain. They would take care to look all around themselves. So one generally walked right past the cottage that resided in the center of the underworld. All manner of herb growing from the pots in the windows and the square, raised gardens around. They were not looking for the obvious, but rather their perception of what this part of the world should be, thereby missing the reality before them.

If she had a name, other than The Oracle, no one knew of it. It had been her definition for so long she did not remember who she was before she was named that. She was fond enough of Osephus to consider him a friend, and she kept that circle small.

She had gotten to know him through the centuries when he would come with Hades. She knew enough of his story to see how he worshipped Hades while being taken for granted. It felt deeper than that though. Humans took the love of their pets for granted, they expected the animal to love them in return for food and water. They only went a small step farther with their offspring. Who were still expected to earn their parents affection with little to know choice in the matter. It seemed to her the concept of free will and unconditional love was something that they were still moving towards evolutionarily.

It was a bit like that with Hades and Osephus, he loved Osephus as the humans their pets, believing Osephus would be remembered that way and that Hades had done him a favor for it.The Oracle had been watching Osephus from the corner of her eye through all of the visits. She took in his whole being while he was there. She was sure that you did not have to be an Oracle to feel his grief, disappointment and underlying anger, more at himself than any one else. Osephus, for the rest of his life, regret his decision to follow and believe Hades, even though he worshipped him.

The Oracle was sitting outside with her herbs when Osephus walked up to her door. Three small cat like creatures lay at her feet looking in the same direction she was. She called them her children, among so many other names that would volley out of her mouth depending on what they were doing.

Despite their mischief, being around them just made you feel good. Like a warm blanket after you were outside in the rain. When they chose to touch you they emitted a type of pheromone that created a euphoria. They chose you though. Despite their small stature they could maul well. Osephus would feel them looking at him, as if they could see into his soul, before they would wander over to pet him. They had free will, the Oracle saw to that. She was very proud of each one of them.

Osephus had made it to the door and asked permission to approach, not from the Oracle but from her pets, they guarded the Oracle with fervor. Osephus had seen what they had done to larger beings than himself, using their free will that he was respecting in the moment.

They fascinated him, being so brave and yet so small, he shivered with envy. The Oracle waved him forward, whispering something to her pets. He asked her about their health and how her herbs were growing while gathering the courage to ask her the real question that he had come to see her for. The Oracle was curious as to why Osephus was alone, he was never there without Hades, could he be in the process of becoming? That would be a process to be privy to for sure.

She knew it must be important for Osephus to be without Hades, at least to Osephus it was. He ran great risk to come there as the Oracle was as much Hades pet as her beautiful children were hers, only they had more free will. Hades did not want to share the power that said pet had and Osephus knew this, so what ever he had to share must be worth the risk of death and wrath of Hades. Her three little darlings meandered over to Osephus, one by one, sharing their gifts, perhaps they had gathered how very little joy that he had in his life.

He was permitted no life outside of the life that he shared with Hades, so todays bravery was a sign of growth he felt.

The Oracle motioned for him to take a seat on one of her stone benches. "What brings me the honor of your visit, a visit form the page of Hades?"

He smiled and nodded graciously, the title not lost on him. He looked away from her gaze, clutching and wringing his hands.

"I have a matter of importance with Hades that Hades does not realize is so important," was blurted out while running the words together.

The Oracle narrowed her eyes. She was all for the under dog in secret, but once she had openly defied a god and he had marred her beauty in remembrance of that day. It had only been a finger, but for her she used those fingers in her divination work. The god had calculated coldly and carefully what would make the deepest impact, he had made the correct choice. Every time she used that hand her ego ached.

Time had not faded that wound so she was in no hurry to incur the wrath of another god, especially Hades who was known for his inventive torture. There was a reason he could stomach being king of the underworld, his tactics of realization to the point. She had seen no small number of beings made examples in creative ways that Hades came up with, ways that no other being would have thought of. She was not about to willingly put herself through some of that.

There was something about the desperation on his face that tugged at her to at least hear him out, and before she had the good sense to stop her self she asked him what he had come to see her about. Osephus raised his dark eyes to meet her golden ones and began telling her the story of Samiel and Sara, explaining that the parties, the festivities that Hades could never get enough of were to drown out how he missed her. He would get so drunk, though, that they always ended in his angry fits of temper, made worse by the reality that she was still not there. Pity the poor fool still in the room with Hades, it took a lot to get him drunk. Often Osephus was the poor fool.

"Can you help me find Sara so that Hades has happiness again?" Osephus asked.

The Oracle had no love for Hades, so his side of the tale did not pull on her heart strings, but Osephus did. She could only imagine what he endured behind closed doors. The fact that he was genuine in wanting Hades to be happy moved her as well, though she surmised some of the want was from self preservation as well.

He continued by stating that he knew the Oracle to be so talented that this would be easy for her, and then perhaps his master would not only cease his tantrums, but be happy. Osephus's face showed the relief that flooded over his being with those last words, and the Oracle felt for him. She asked a few more questions about Sara while standing up, appreciating what Osephus was trying to do. The fact that Hades had a weakness was powerful knowledge, she made a guess that Osephus, and now herself, were the only two that knew. Osephus had brought it to her not as an act of power, he could have, but from a tired soul that wanted relief from the decades of tyranny.

"All right then," she clapped her hands together, "we will take a look at what the guides have to say."

Osephus followed her through the stone entryway into what he called the room of wonders, she called it her divination room. Not one piece of furniture matched in her whole house, but they were all made of different, stunning woods, to keep her grounded, she would remark. Her room of wonders was a round room in the very center of her house, with bookcases for walls and a large, wooden table in the center.

The room was cluttered with books, herbs and crystals. At the very top of the vaulted ceiling looked like a small sun, you could not look at it directly so it was difficult to know for certain. The underworlds temperature as well as darkness was not conducive to growing life, even the Oracles. When Hades had first taken her she had faded quickly, needing the light and warmth to continue her connection to those things that others could not see, so Hades made a deal with Zeus and Zeus formed a lighting bolt, keeping it in a stage of stasis that gave warmth and light for the Oracle and her ways.

Many of the shelves had books but almost as many had what she called her tools of divination, such as crystals, runes, tuning forks, shells, and a host of things that she had created and not yet named but used. She had told him once that there was a message in the way that the leaves fall on an autumn day, if you only know how to read the language that was written on it's very veins as we are all connected.

Osephus did not feel connected to anything, but out of gratitude he would not tell her this small fact. She was gathering some stones, runes she called them, and one of her special lay cloths. She then used a smudge stick to cleanse the space that they were in.

How you can cleanse anything in the underworld was beyond Osephus, it felt like too much nothingness for there to be anything that would be large enough to make a difference. The Oracle looked at him as he thought this, he shuffled nervously, could she read minds also? It did feel different when she was done, he would give her that.

There were three doors that entered into the Oracles work room. Osephus had noticed in the past when he had been there with Hades that once the Oracle had cleansed, her children would sit, one in each door way. Today he decided to ask her about that, why not?

He felt bold in his moment of courage. He straightened himself a little taller in his chair, "Oracle, why do your children sit in the doorway while you do this?"

"They are much more than what they appear to be," she said, while glancing at them lovingly. "They can see what the naked eye cannot see in any dimension. As I call in guidance they keep out any extra, unwanted guidance from those dimensions, that may wander in after a good cleansing. I ask for the best, the highest form of guidance and protection, even in the underworld but it would be no surprise to find out that the underworld carries a large population of unhappy spirits that would like to cause trouble. Energy follows intention, even in the darkness of this place. I choose to carry a higher energy and my children help keep this possible in the middle of a darkness that would swallow one whole."

Osephus let his gaze rest on the first one, Kye. He was sitting in the nearest doorway. They were the size of a humans small house cat. Their eyes were massive, looking far too large for their head with slits for pupils, they had three tails fashioned along their spine like dominoes. Come to think of it, he wondered how they did not get them tangled up.

Kye was a little larger than the other two. The Oracle would never say that she had a favorite, but he slept on the pillow beside her head, so we will leave that where it is. It was difficult to say what color Kye was. At first glance he looked like a murky brown, but when he came near to touch you, it looked like the very hair would turn on the root and waves of a deep purple would appear. He was tiny but fierce for sure.

The second one was Onie. She was the color of taffy when it was still warm. Osephus had taffy once, one of the few pleasures Hades had allowed him. He especially liked Onie because she brought back that memory so vividly. He squinted at her, perhaps that was one

31

of the strange things they did to aid the Oracle, bringing happy memories to mind.

The third one was called Callod. He was the color of seaweed on the tide. He was also the least friendly of the three and would stare. It sounds petty, the staring, but he did not blink. And he just kept doing it, nonstop. Osephus looked away, best to leave them to do whatever creepiness they were doing in the moment.

The Oracle was unwrapping some red stone with what looked like inscriptions on them. They look like glass fire. Carnelian, she had told him, to help find the king of the underworlds passion they would use golden fire. The inscriptions were runic symbols.

"So I can hear the guides better," she whispered.

It only took her a moment to gather this and that and then she began. Osephus loved every bit of this part. She lit candles, played bells and burned strange smelling things. Clearing the area she called it. That was probably a good idea, Osephus thought to himself. Then she would go through similar rituals and finally call upon the guides, as she called whatever spoke to her through her trinkets.

Her eyes narrowed Uh huh, uh huh, hmm. Osephus sat up more. He was not getting a good feeling about where this was going. The Oracle's face scrunched up more. She let out a sigh, more like a gust of wind from her face, and she said no one can find Sarah.

What?? How does heaven and hell lose a being? How do you misplace a soul? The Oracle was perplexed. Moving more stones around while chanting under her breath.

Somehow Hade's love had completely disappeared. Osephus slumped in his seat, realizing that he had better get away before it was found he had been here. All of his visions of grandeur still glittering in the red stones in front of him as the reality slowly hit him square in the face, that if caught he would have nothing to barter with. He thanked the Oracle and scurried off.

The Oracle was so intent on the perplexity of the knowledge that was being told to her that she did not notice his departure. How can no one know where a soul was? It was simply because Sarah had fallen. She had ached for Hade's, her Samiel.

She had heard the tales and the stories. He needed her. But Sarah was a being of light and when she set her intention to fall so great was her light, and love of that light, that when she fell she did not fall far.

She hung in between the heaven and the Earth. Holding to that which she loved while falling to he who she loved. In that moment of deep, incredible intention, Sarah became what we all know as the morning star. In between both of her lives, while still shining for the universe to see and feel her light.

PART THREE

Somewhere between there and now,

I am waiting, ignoring why and how.

I am guiding other souls to a world of wonder and delight,

as the thoughts of you give radiance to my light.

I am passing on my love for you,

in the moments that nothing else will do.

Because my soul does not think another day may pass

before I see your face, your touch, at last.

So I will hang here, somewhere between the there and now.

Waiting, always for you, ignoring the why and how,

in the knowledge, that as our morning dawns,

to each other, once again we will be drawn.

In the ecstasy and pain, that many disdain,

called love.

For many years Sarah clung to the sky, exploding with her love for creation. Guiding travelers and pilgrims through the dark. At first, it was glorious, and in the beginning she had forgotten her origin.

"Every time we fall we forget just a little more of where we came from and why we came. We forget what made us decide to take this crazy ride on a spinning ball," she had been told by an angel previous to her fall.

After a few millennia of shining she felt odd. So odd. Like a piece of her was missing. As if it had just fallen away and she needed to find it. Slowly, ever slowly, she remembered everything. As the memories flickered over her nebula being, she felt her light dim. She had enjoyed being a light in the dark but she missed Samiel deeply.

She knew she would never find him here in this moment that she had chosen to hang in between worlds. She knew in the middle of who she was that she would have to fall again. She thought about what the other Angel had said about how each time it takes us a little longer to remember where we came from.

That made her nervous and put a small amount of hesitation in her determination, but then that old ache would crawl across her belly again and so she would acknowledge that she wanted nothing more than to be with Samiel. She need to set her intentions closer to where he would be. So after a time of leading travelers and pilgrims through the darkness, Sarah set her intention once again to be with her beloved Samiel, determined to give it her all, she fell. This time she was born, reborn, as a daughter of Oceanus, god of the sea.

She had been unsure of just how to set her intention, or where, rather. She had heard stories of what had become of Samiel but her light heart did not want to fully believe them. What did register was that he was a god among men, so a god is what she needed to set that intention for.

That is how she became part of a god's life, just not the one she was looking for. She was born Luece, daughter of Oceanus, water nymph of the oceans. What the other angel told her was correct, she did not remember who she was. At least not for a very, very, long time. But that, dear reader, was a blessing. There was no deep longing in her for a piece that felt like it was missing. Because she did not remember such a thing. The saltwater was her domain, her kingdom. She was the youngest of the eight of Oceana's daughters and his most beloved.

Old age had softened the Titan. And Luece was so easy to love. Hair as white as the ocean foam. Eyes the color of the sky after a storm. Skin as pale as the seashells she lovingly recycled. That was Luece.

She would sing for him and let me tell you a nymph can sing. Their voices have a magical intonation that captivates their listener, drawing them in and holding them on each note as if they became the song themselves. In the moment of the music all you are is who you were meant to become. Many a human sailor lost their course not because Luece was some evil sea creature but because in that moment, that melody ,sailor, pirate, traveler, all were caught in the oneness of who they were on the notes of her song and they would lose their way the moment the song stopped.

It is a strong person indeed who has worked out who they are enough to always be that person. So many that would hear and feel her song did not have the strength to continue being themselves. Many of the evil stories of sea lore come from Luece singing so many years ago, her song carried in the wind and on the waves.

Oceanus would call for her, especially in the moments that he had to make a great decision and the weight of it was just too great to bear. Luece would come and sit at the Titan's feet and sing her song. His fears would clear like the clouds at dawn and his sun would appear with the light and answer that he needed. To say that Luece was dear to him, well there was not a word invented for what that daughter meant to him and all the world knew this.

Luece's world, as well as Oceanus's world ,was about to be changed in a way neither would have ever dreamed of, causing a ripple throughout time that is still felt today but seldom spoken of or remembered, as the tale was not as popular as Zeus's mighty lightning bolts or Hades chariot of fear or even the ferry man of death. That guy still has T shirts made and people are still trying to get around his toll road, to no avail, I might add.

So, in order to finish Luece's tale, we must go back to the Oracle's house in the Underworld, where she had, off and on through the years, tried to find Sarah through her gift of divination. She knew Sarah still was alive while she was the morning star. She just could not find where Sarah was, as she had never experienced this before she was very unfamiliar with the terminology the universe was using while they repeatedly tried to tell her where Sara was while she was the morning star. These things were truly lost in translation.

Meanwhile, Osephus had brainstormed for a decade or so and had come to the conclusion that Hades thought Sarah was special so they just needed someone else that was special. He, Osephus, would find someone special for Hades. Then maybe Hades fits of anger and spontaneous combustion would then cease to exist.

Poor Osephus. He did not realize what path Hades had set his feet on. What atrocities Hades would have to give an account for. Love from others cannot heal such things. Though for most of us we fumble around with this one for a minute.

It is love for ourselves that carries us through such things. Love for ourselves that brings us to who we are and who we are meant to be. And Hades self loathing at himself when he had moments of realization of how he had attained his power, well, those

39

moments were stronger than the love he had for Sarah. They were fed, every so often, with the proof that he would supply to them. Hades increasingly labeled different things as "weakness." Thereby building more of a wall around his heart that he had long ago stopped taking care of.

So Osephus set off to find the perfect mate for Hades while the Oracle continued to check in with her guidance system on Sarah. Osephus knew there would be nothing in the Underworld that Hades would consider beautiful. As dark as Hades was, Osephus had noticed his taste in the opposite sex was normally the lighter beings. They usually had to be subdued to be with Hades so it was generally an unpleasant experience for everyone but Hades.

Osephus shuffled his feet. The lighter the beings were, the less time they lasted in the darkness of the Underworld. It was as if Hades wanted them and then was ashamed of wanting them. The poor soul had been taken from the only home in life they knew, and just did not last long in the darkness of the Underworld. The females of the Underworld were ruthless. They were Hades playthings at times while also serving whatever wistful creature of light that was amongst them.

Osephus shivered and then clapped his hands together, no sense dwelling on negative memories of the past. He would find someone stronger, someone as strong as Hades. Oh dear, that would most likely be a God like Hades. Which would be a goddess, of course, he was glad at times that no one seemed able to read his thoughts.

Well, he could not capture a God, or a goddess, has he had other beings. He tapped his head. Sometimes this sped up his thinking process, he felt. Well first, he had to find a goddess that was not taken. Then he would worry about the rest of it all.

He shuffled off to find Hades, who was in his great room reclined on his seat with a ledger over his face. With power comes bookwork Osephus had noticed. He tiptoed to see if the master was sleeping. You did not want to wake him or you would have the possibility of being fed to his hellhound Cerberus.

As much as Osephus loved the Oracle's cat like creatures, he hated Cerberus. The Hellhound would often be slinking in different places watching everything that was going on with his three heads and six pairs of eyes that seemed to shift to every corner of the world. Osephus had wondered how even with three heads Cerberus saw so much and could be so many places. At the current moment he lay off to the side of his master's chair.

Osephus stood awkwardly off to the side for what seemed like a significant amount of time when Hades moved slightly and the ledger fell off of his face. Immediately Osephus felt his soul naked, stripped of anything good, as Hades met his eyes. Osephus had been practicing this moment repeatedly in his mind.

Hades had another festival coming up. He would need special things from the world above. He, Osephus, was here to offer himself a tribute to gather said things. Hades waved him off, slightly acknowledging what was said. That was enough for Osephus. His normal shuffle turned into a sprint as he headed topside to find his master's happiness.

There were certain places the gods and goddesses frequented. He would start with the nearest glade. The sun was mid sky when he emerged from the Underworld. He pulled his cloak around his pale being, the paleness of his skin almost immediately gave away his origin.

Not being used to such light was a challenge as his senses adjusted to the brightness and warmth. He remembered, very faintly now, when he was an angel and seeing all of this creation excited him. There were so many possibilities in that moment of what creation would become and of himself, what he would become. He quickened

41

his pace, no sense dwelling on what could have been. He was in the very present moment and in order for it to improve, the faster he found a lovely goddess, the better.

Poor Osephus, he never really thought it through. The goddesses were every bit as proud as the gods. Hades respect of the opposite sex was so lacking over the years that Osephus had grown accustomed to the thought that women were less than a man. Had he payed closer attention he would have noted that Hades treated everyone the same, male and female, he treated him both equally less than himself.

Before Osephus had left on his little quest he had visions of the goddess's jumping at the chance to be with the mighty Hades. These visions were soon replaced by the reality that Hades wasn't as big top side as he was in the dark. Osephus rubbed his chin at the difference.

So far he had approached three of the goddesses handmaids. Never once, before he set out, would he have thought of the replies that he had been given. The first handmaid never stopped gathering herbs for her mistress. During the conversation she barely touched Osephus with her gaze, her reply a simple snort. The other two, well, he wished it had merely been a snort. His face still burned from a slap and his clothes were ruined from wearing someone's meal. Most definitely not what he expected.

He brushed himself off and stopped by a stream to wash his face a bit. That would bruise later for sure, he thought as he rubbed his face. He did his best to remove the food so that he would look somewhat presentable.

He heard laughter in the distance. Female laughter. Now, in the days that Osephus walked the Earth as Osephus, there were certain places that only the gods and goddesses went. Humans that served them did not trespass on such holy ground. Even though it was holy because the humans made it that way with their need to worship anything other than themselves. They would tell bedtime stories to each other from one generation to the next of the origin of their self worth or lack of self worth, the next generation felt even less capable than the first to think for themselves or believe in themselves for that matter. They had the same powers as the gods laying latent inside of them but due to a belief of lack, they never realized that they each carried inside of themselves their very own divinity.

Osephus paused his thoughts as heard laughter once again. He felt hope as he knew only goddesses would be in this glade. Glancing up he saw two goddesses, laughing and gathering flowers. He squinted to see better, best to be quiet as he was not with his master.

Perhaps they had a servant he could speak with. He crept closer, his eyes sparkled as he recognized the goddesses the closer that he became. Hair the color of acorns that fell in waves off of her shoulders, eyes the color of the Atlantic ocean right after a storm, the one nearest to him was the older of the two. The only reason Osephus could even tell that was because he knew who she was. Demeter was her name, she was the wife of Zeus. The other woman would have to be Persephone then, her daughter.

Osephus had heard many stories of Persephone. She was very beautiful in person, he thought her stories were just. Hair the color of cocoa and eyes to match with an Olive complexion. The shape of her body, well Osephus had never been with a woman in a carnal way, but she definitely stirred something in him.

That was his lot in this life, at least for this life it seemed, no woman, but Persephone was so much of a goddess his heart did a wee dance of excitement in his chest. She would be perfect for his master! Her beauty and grace surpassed that of the other goddesses by far. He had also heard that the daughter of Zeus could hold her own in conversation as she was well studied in the arts. Hades would get bored in conversation easily if there was nothing to challenge his mind.

He glanced frantically around. There had to be a handmaiden of some sort nearby. The wife and daughter of Zeus would demand it.

There!! He spotted her off to the far left under a large tree, she was preparing them a meal, he sighed, hoping that he would not wear this one. Osephus took care to make a wide birth around the goddesses they did not take kindly to servants interrupting their time.

As he got closer he saw their hand maiden glancing from the corner of her eye while she worked. Being as they were in The Valley of the gods he was not worried that she would be too alarmed. As was mentioned earlier one did not just meander through such a place. She would know that he was in some way connected to the gods.

He approached her slowly, his dark eyes trying to hide the excitement welling inside of him, while he rolled his master plan around in his head. She did not look directly at him until he was right in front of her. He introduced himself, which she then did in turn.

She was Dahlia, servant to the goddesses and what did he want, she asked while looking as her work. Her initial shortness did not disturb him as he understood the haste she felt in getting everything ready in a timely fashion. Silly gods and goddesses, they wanted things done by yesterday. He shared his ingenious plan of uniting their master and mistress asking if Dahlia would help him accomplish this. He explained that at the end of this great plan they would obviously be exalted for their efforts and accomplishments.

Dahlia snorted, knowing that her mistress had no desire to be owned by any God. That's what happened to the goddesses, she thought, they lost their identity of what they were goddesses of and became the wife of God so-and-so, taking on that persona instead of their own, unique gifts. No, Persephone would not be part of that and Demeter, wife of Zeus, would not allow what was taken from her to be taken from her beautiful daughter.

This was not what Osephus was expecting at all. There was not one ounce of excitement from Dahlia. Quite the opposite really. Dahlia had looked disgusted as she explained all of this to him. Hades really! Dahlia snorted again. Of all the gods, Persephone would not live in that darkness of an Underworld!

Perhaps at that moment, had no assumptions been made by Osephus, with clarity being the choice verb for that day, our story would not take such a dark loop of a cul-de-sac in history. But wars have been started on lesser assumptions. Osephus assumed Demeter simply did not want Persephone to marry. It was as if he heard, "blah blah, Demeter said no," and absolutely nothing in between those words.

He thanked Dahlia graciously. She looked puzzled, then shook her head and went on about her business. She had heard many things from serving the goddesses about Hades and his most trusted servant Osephus. Even she did not have the blind faith that he did and her mistresses were far more giving than Hades. Hades gave his hell hound more love than any other living being, despite Osephus being so faithful. She would not wish that upon anyone. No, the God of the Underworld had created his persona, now he could waltz with it, as he liked to do at all of the gatherings of the gods.

Osephus hurried off, his mind churning with different routes of uniting his master with his new found mistress. If he could get Persephone alone he could tell her of his masters good qualities, that wouldn't even take much of her time. They were not many, but Osephus felt what Hades lacked in quantity he had in quality.

He shook his head in puzzlement. Even if Demeter were away, which, come to think of it, Demeter was not very often away from Persephone, in fact he had never seen Persephone without Demeter, it would be death for someone like Osephus to approach a goddess. He straightened, it would be a noble death of honor for his master. Then reality washed over him.

He didn't really want to die a noble death, or any other way of death, for that matter. He walked slowly through The Valley of the gods. The sun was in the middle of the sky, the sweet flowers waved on the midday breeze. But Osephus was lost in the circle that his mind had created. Hades missed Sara, no one could find Sara, so a goddess would have to do.

One cannot just swoop in and take a goddess, or could one? He stopped dead in his tracks. He had seen Hades do this very thing, collect goddesses. Well, Hades called them "the lesser than" because they were, in his eyes, barely goddesses. They were the daughters of gods and goddesses yes, but had a human as one parent, they were referred to as demigods. It was as if you almost made it to the finals, but not quite, maybe next time.

Hades had been known to help himself to such goddesses and by that I mean that he just took them. Somewhere Hades had completely forgotten and lost the concept of free will. If he wanted something, the mighty Hades took it.

Deep inside Hades still lay the love for the things he and Sara had shared together . The moments of creation, the joy of birth, the wonder of the beauty that even a spider's web held. He still felt these things, but the enchantment of a beautiful woman was difficult for him to resist, so he just didn't resist it. He did this more at public events. Especially those hosted by humans.

Sometimes he feigned that it was because he expected a toll of sorts for the Underworld. Osephus always let a snort at this toll. Those coming to the Underworld had chosen that for themselves . Believing their whole lives that they could attain to nothing else. They paid that toll themselves while they were alive, living in a hell in their head. Never needing anything at all from Hades.

The illusion that he had created around himself was most impressive. So when he blustered of toll and people thought of an uncomfortable afterlife of where they no doubt would end up, well the king of the Underworld could have whatever he asked for. There were many of his concubines that inhabited the Underworld just this way.

Osephus scratched his chin, his dark eyes clouded over. Those were demi goddesses. The daughter of Zeus did not fall into that category. Just being the mixture of Demeter and Zeus kept Persephone at an intimidating distance from any of the gods.

He quickened his step. Hades had business with the Oracle this afternoon. Osephus would bring this matter before her as soon as Hades left. It would simply look like Osephus stayed to clean up.

Back through the gates of the Underworld he ran. Feeling the unhappiness of so many lost souls hit him all at once. Lost because they had never realized in life who they were, not realizing the abilities that they carried inside of them while rejecting their own magnificence. He rounded on the oracle's cabin, almost missing it out of the corner of his eye.

Kye sat in the doorway, his three tails slowly waving erratically. Osephus was made almost dizzy by the way he moved them. He shook his head and sighed, realizing the creature was creating his own form of cat and mouse. Osephus straightened, asking with a tone of respect if the creature in front of him would let him pass. Kye looked him dead in the eyes following what he felt was a soul sweep and then moved out of the doorway, brushing against Osephus, and literally gracing him with his presence.

Osephus could hear Hades voice from the center room that had all of the doors. He slunk into a bench off to the side. The only acknowledgment of his presence was the flick of the Oracle's eye in his direction, she knew for both their sakes not to take her attention off of Hades. He demanded your full attention in his presence and had people taken care of immediately for a lack in this area concerning him.

It was difficult to tell time in the Underworld. The darkness seemed to creep into all of the corners, even into the corners of time. Where above in the light you could almost feel when it was time for the sun to let itself go down, not so here. Time was abstract in the whole scheme of the experience.

Kye nudged Osephus foot, he had fallen asleep and this startled him. Hades had stood, he was done asking the question of the guides that the Oracle spoken with. He was looking at conquering some new corners of the world and without the oracle's advice he would not delve into certain areas. He still remembered where he came from and though he was egotistical and self serving he still knew that to remain a god he needed help. Osephus stood up and the Oracle asked if Hades would be so kind as to let her have Osephus help while she regained her strength from such a visit. Hades hesitated, his eyes resting on the oracle's face. This was a new request but he had no reason to deny her.

Osephus almost sighed too loudly in his relief at the Oracle taking such a move. It was quiet for a few minutes while Osephus waited to make sure Hades was indeed gone . He told the Oracle everything that had passed since he had last seen her and of the beautiful Persephone. His question was how to get the two of them together?

The Oracle took a deep breath, wondering at her lack of brains to even visit such a request. But she knew that Osephus asked from a place of love, so the Oracle cast her runes and asked the guides what the best course of action was. The guidance that came was for Hades to simply ask Zeus for Persephone's hand in marriage.

Osephus was pleased, that did not seem too difficult! The Oracle, however, knew that this would not be easy, Hades was proud and arrogant, taking without asking. He felt he was owed anything that came his way. Becoming more grounded in this belief the longer time went and the less he remembered who he was. She knew that for him to ask Zeus would be no small task because he would have to face some truths about himself and Hades did not walk such a path as that.

She tried to explain this to Osephus who was being pleasantly petted by Kye. It looked as though Kye felt responsible for Osephus being in the room and was attempting to alleviate the heaviness he felt radiating off of his mistress. Osephus simply could not hear what she was saying. She frowned at Kye, he hesitated before brushing once more, a long pheromone stroke against Osephus and then disappearing around a corner.

Osephus, still dazed, tried to grasp what the Oracle was trying to tell him. Hades and Zeus, known as brothers, had been old comrades in the fall . Many of the gods in power had banned their talents together to hold the places they did, but you will notice that none of them are exactly roomies. Staying in the vicinity too long of each other affected the weather. Literally, Zeus would get upset, and well, he wasn't the god of thunder for nothing. Once they climbed to the heights they so thought they wanted to attain, they met only when necessary and that was usually at a human function or because of humans. Every once in a while a human would remember its connection with the divine, where it truly came from, and then it would get the wild thought of saving/changing the world.

Osephus rolled his black eyes. That was always fun. The extremities that the gods would then go to as they played cat and mouse with said human, well, it was exhausting. He shook the last of Kye's pheromone off and truly focused on what the Oracle was saying. It's sunk in. She was right.

The mighty Hades was not going to have Zeus to dinner and ask for the god's daughters hand in marriage. There would have to be another way. He thought of the women Hades had, remembering how they all came to be in the presence of Hades. How they all now chose to stay in the Underworld as his concubines rather than live in the knowledge that they were one of his fleeting addictions.

Persephone's beautiful face flitted through his mind, he knew that she very well would face that same ending but she was so lovely surely that would be the spark needed for Hades to fuel what Sara made him feel so many centuries earlier. Poor Osephus. Love does not work that way, when we love truly love someone, even if we forget that love, that fire it still burns in our hearts and chests, keeping the beacon lit in hopes that the one we were so in love with will one day come home. Osephus could not know that in Hades heart that beacon was a mighty fire kindled only for his light. Waiting to see hers burn through his darkness. There was not a beautiful woman that could hold the same flame that his Sara did.

PART FOUR

I lost myself in the dark of pain, and reached for what I thought true.

Moving in the motions of time, painting over the bruise.

The wounds of life, the wounds of love, carried in our veins,

ripping with intensity, with the ugly face of strain,

teach us deeper, farther, lies the glory of the soul,

lost in Stardust, crushed, never again whole.

Galaxy's were made from the tears of one so lost

so I hang my nebula in the sky to remind me of such cost,

that what lines the night is not the sun of day

but our broken, crushed stars, left to guide the way.

Hades paced his large chamber where Cerberus lay, two of his six eyes on his master, at the drafty hearth. Architectural structuring was not a strong point in the Underworld. Hades had awoken to feeling that same old pain. He had been dreaming of her, of Sara, it happened less and less as time went on but every so often he would have dreams, remembrances of Sara.

He would awaken to the memory of her voice, her excitement at something that she had created. He would dream of her eyes, alight with the excitement of all the possibilities of what could be. In that dream he would relive the feeling of love he felt near her. It was not only the remembrance of her love but the remembrance of who he was before he committed the atrocities to be where he is now. His face softened and he halted as he remembered Sara, bent over an idea of creation, her energy reaching what must have been the corners of the universe as she explained it to him and her enthusiasm. This had been his dream that he had just awoken from. The glorious remembrance of a moment of pure joy.

He picked up the closest thing to him, it was a book, and threw it with a heave that it shook the room on impact. He did not want to feel this. He had looked for her and decided that Sara did not want him or she would have come with him. Hades had never admitted the rejection and abandonment he had felt by Sara not coming with him. But throughout the centuries it had grown like a thorn in his side towards Sara.

After all, we are all the same, even the gods we have christened. It is so much easier to look outside of ourselves, to blame anything other than our own decision making for the moments we find ourselves in in life, be they good or bad. Hades would then get angry on such a day when the feelings would get the best of him, when the memories of Sara would tickle in the back of his mind. When every instance of the day would make him question how she would react or think. He would become more aware of his inner dialogue, shake it off, and then try to bury it in one of his several addictions.

In as much as he loved Sara, he had grown to hate her just a smidge as she had become the inner voice of compassion and empathy in his life and he definitely did not need such things to accomplish being the king of the Underworld. He sat and lay his face in his hands, he had to snap out of this, it was a busy day and he could not have this fog of love/hatred swirling about his brain for a woman that he most likely would never see again.

As the fate would have it Osephus chose that moment to be brave, ever so brave, for one moment of his life. He had formed what he felt an ingenious full proof plan for his master's happiness. Had it been any other day Hades would have laughed him out of the room but the fates had parted the way for Osephus to have his very own moment of glory.

Osephus picked up on his master's mood as he walked in, he took a deep breath and barreled through what he had to say before the vibe of the room made him realize that imminent death could be a possibility for today's disclosure. He described Persephone, explaining whose daughter she was, nonchalantly mentioning how she frequent-ed the Valley of the gods and what her schedule, per her handmaiden was. Osephus had talked this over with Oracle, she was skeptical at best, but liked Osephus and did not want to see harm come to him, so she had helped go over what to say and how to act so as not to make Hades suspicious. As Osephus spoke, he moved diligently around the room, straightening and tidying as he went, to make it seem as if he was simply gossiping. Hopefully it looked like he was straightening with a vigor, as sweat was dripping down from his temples.

He mentioned how he had wandered through the Valley of the gods on one of his errands for Hades. He described seeing Demeter.

Hades perked up a bit at this, the wife of Zeus was usually a hot topic. Then he described Persephone, he now had Hades full attention.

The fates were definitely with Osephus, he plunged deeper, leaving tidbits of gossip like dog hair from Cerberus as he went about the room. This peaked Hades interest greatly. He did not remember Osephus talking about a women, well, ever, and they have been together for several centuries, since before the fall.

That's all that it took for the mighty Hades to fall for the goddess Persephone, sight unseen, was the faith of his servant. Too bad Hades never told Osephus, it would have been good for dear old Osephus to have known all the effort and work put in was meticulously well accepted. Hades had hung on every word and now knew the daily comings and goings of Persephone.

His manservant had painted such a picture that Hades felt he must see exactly what Osephus saw. It would help, if he could not have Sara, and he was most definitely bored with what he did have. This was truly uncharacteristic of Osephus to go on and on about a female, especially a goddess. Hades slammed his hand down on the great armchair that he was resting in, Cerberus jumped, though one head remained sleeping. Nasty hound, Osephus thought, as he was collecting himself back together. He could not read Hades and was so afraid that the gesture was made in frustration.

It was not, it was made in determination. Hades was poor at reading the room, though empathetic qualities were not even a weak point with Hades, in fact they just weren't a point at all. He jumped up, Cerberus followed, and strode out with determination.

Osephus, his whole life after the fall, had been taught nothing but to be wary of the next beating, whether it be physical, verbal or mental. He woke up with a subconscious knowing every morning that the first would come, he had spent so many years experiencing this that as time went on he just lived in a realm of fight or flight, as many of us do. Just waiting for the next bad experience, expecting the fates to line it up as lessons for our own specific person. Osephus never realized that he had the opportunity to write his own story, to create his own fate .

At this time in Osephus life, though, that would be quite difficult, almost a rewriting of his cellular makeup, as traumas had been his great companion from the moment he fell. Choosing to follow someone else instead of his own voice, his own truth. What had he done today? Why had he told Hades all of this, he should have left well enough alone!

He sat down, then paced, then repeated the last two steps. He had not seen Hades with such a look on his face. Had he angered him with his words? What would the repercussions be? This sick dread bubbled in his stomach physically. He would have to deal with the physical repercussions of this first before he moved to work through the mental. Poor Osephus had several days of worry and dread before he was privy to the truth of the matter.

Hades had strode off to The Valley of the gods, he had never gave a report to Osephus of his comings and goings before so it certainly never crossed his mind today. He perhaps would have said something had he known the internal battle that Osephus was facing. Hades cared for Osephus in his own way.

Once, so long ago before the fall, they had been comrades, equals and friends. At times when Sara would float through his mind he would remember the days of comradery with Osephus and creating. His heart would then grow soft towards Osephus with the memories.

Those times became less and less as he rose in power and worship. Osephus was simply no longer his equal and systems were in place for a reason. He knew this because he had helped create the system.

As Hades was a poor reader of rooms he would have been hard pressed to feel Osephus current state of tragedy, though. Hades picked up speed, from his vast Underworld he rose through the gates, into the sun of day, blinding him a bit in the process. The Underworld had light, marvelous crystal light. But it, even for all of its beauty, could not match the light and warmth of the sun. Hades paused for a moment while he grew accustomed to the change. Slowly his vision adjusted. The Valley of the gods lay before him.

Sometimes he felt a bit angry when he came out into the light. King of the Underworld had not been his original aspiration when he began his journey here. He had enjoyed creating enough to realize all life on this planet needed just a few things. Sunlight being one of them.

Sure, he was the god of lost souls, feared, revered, but he was still in the flesh and blood. The god's age slowly, very slowly. They put a lot of thought into all of this before they fell and while they were doing a little extra creating, like two more tablespoons of butter in grandma's cake recipe, they thought that more butter would make it better. Right?

No, no that is terribly wrong. Butter makes it better but not too much butter. That just gives you diarrhea. Hades had added too much butter. His need for power, that insistent drive that he had felt to control everything, had blinded him to so many things. One of the biggest being that he could have made his life one of splendor and glory. The fears that entangled the neurons in his brain, fear that he would lose this power that he had worked so hard to gain. This twisted his perception. As time went on it became a little more twisted in his efforts to attain more power.

In his mind he realized the Underworld was not the glory that Zeus had but Zeus had more love than fear from creation. Hades had fear, sure that was lonely he thought to himself, but fear was where real power was. Fear would drive a man to madness, never love.

The people that wrote that love drove them to madness, well it was because they were afraid of loosing that love. Blah, he thought, it was never the love, it just did not lead to that destination, it was always the fear of losing that love that drove man to madness. Zeus could keep his lightning bolts thunder and splendor. The Underworld, and fear of that darkness crept through every heart, that was the seat of power, he shivered in his mind of glory as he quickened his pace to where Osephus said Persephone would be.

The willows hung over the river that flowed through The Valley. They're branches swaying back-and-forth as the breeze tapped them each gently. To the left Hades saw a group of willows with three women sitting underneath.

He recognized Demeter, her hair the color of an acorn, green eyes dancing with the glory of her day. The wife of Zeus was always up for merriment Hades thought. He had secretly wanted her at his side, not for her beauty, though she was stunning, no, for her mind and her vibration.

She vibrated power and joy. She never would have survived in the darkness of the Underworld. She had considered Hades request, as she did not come into her place of being by being a bystander. But she knew in the depths of her soul the Underworld would snuff out the light that she had so long kept burning inside herself through some of the manipulation she had maneuvered to be in the place that she was at.

Her hair was pulled up as Dahlia placed flowers, woven throughout the braid she created, forming a beautiful crown on her head. Persephone's jet black hair hung to her waist, she lifted her dark eyes to meet Hades. Her eyes feeling as if they were piercing through to his soul, brilliant against her olive skin and black hair.

His heart experienced something he had not felt as her eyes caught you in their gaze, holding you, like when you shake someone's hand and you squeeze on the end, you know, to make sure you know they can grip. Hades gathered himself but before he could speak Demeter rose.

The goddess of harvest knew by the look on Hades face what he was coming to harvest and on first glance she would not commit her daughter to be Queen of that madness. Just to sit on a throne built of guilt and darkness, wrapped in lies told by ourselves and others. That was not a throne for her Persephone. Hades was trying not to stare boldly at Persephone's eyes, he already had an affinity for dark eyes. Such strength he felt radiating from Persephone's.

He and Demeter exchanged pleasantries before she introduced him to the daughter of Zeus. Once Dahlia had finished Demeter's hair she had started on Persephone's hair, weaving it into two braids, just attached at the nape of her neck in one gloricus braid. Demeter rose, almost taller than Hades, and bowed graciously towards him.

"Would you like to share our noon meal?" she gestured at the food Dahlia had lain out.

That afternoon Hades, Lord of our fears and doubts, felt many emotions that were akin to his heaven on Earth. Intelligence, with beauty and grace, he felt, had been lost with some of the arts. And yet here before him was an epiphany of creation in the form of this being.

The sun was setting. Demeter rose prompting Hades of the time. How had the afternoon passed so swiftly? He gathered all of his charm in his parting with Persephone and made his way back to the underworld.

Demeter turned to Persephone, her eyes slightly narrowing as she paused in her perception of what her daughter's thoughts and actions may imply. Persephone's eyes followed Hades as the silhouette became smaller. She had woven a name for herself, though her own title was not as bold as being the daughter of Zeus.

She had so far climbed to as high as she alone could climb. To acquire more power she would need to take on assistance. Hades was definitely not ugly. Jet black hair shoulder length and thick. Eyes as black as what they said his soul was. She had noticed the dim light that glimmered in those handsome eyes and she wondered what or who still lit that light . Overall the whole experience intrigued her.

Demeter was disturbed. She knew her daughter's passion for power but she also knew that Persephone had no idea how truly horrific the darkness can twist one's person's soul. Especially living in that darkness.

The beautiful stones that glowed throughout the Underworld, for all of their beauty and magic, could not replicate the warmth and glory of the sun. Demeter knew that Persephone's lust for power would cloud the goddess's mind on exactly what Hades may want to offer her. Demeter had once been led by Hades lullaby as well, she knew a bit of what her daughter was feeling. There was a special air about Hades, as if fun had just met no boundaries and they rode off that way. Demeter immediately began forming a plan in her head to keep her Persephone from making such a grave error in judgment.

As they wandered out of The Valley of the gods not one word was mentioned of Hades between the two goddesses. The very silence of the Lord of the Underworld was a defining omen of what would then play out because of him.

Hades found his way to The Valley of the gods more frequently in the coming weeks. Then it became daily. Demeter had pressed the matter with Zeus, as she knew that she was no match for Hades, but Zeus always brushed her off.

"He will come to me to ask for her, I will say no and that will be that." Demeter knew in her heart that it would not be that easy. She saw what went on under the willows.

Hades, ever so brilliant in acquiring what he wanted. How he felt his brilliance shine when it was being challenged by something he may not have. He had watched Demeter, almost as much as Persephone, throughout his courtship of the goddess. He knew that she was as leery of him as much as his pride was wounded still from Demeter's rejection.

He had carefully assessed where he may have gone wrong with Demeter after the fact, and was prepared to modify that for the lovely Persephone. Her eyes still captivating him, holding him yet pushing him away as they daily discussed world matters. Her conversation was refreshing to him. He had honestly started this as a boost to his boredom , his ego. A replacement for the void he felt without Sara.

But then, as he got to know Persephone, as he sat or lay under the willows, he began to memorize the angle of her face, the direction of her eyebrow through certain topics. The intonation of her voice became a type of intoxication for him and the Lord of the underworld fell in love.

Persephone, she too, had gone day after day, prepared to accept an offer she felt coming. Not because she felt Hades a worthy lover but because she wanted to be Queen of the underworld. What a title to be respected! What power at the tables she sat at would then become hers!

But as time went on, it too was no longer for what she stayed. It was for moments that his hand brushed hers, his eyes watching her lips as she told tales of Zeus's evening court meetings. The laughter they also shared over such meetings. It was genuine, and felt in each other's beings. They were in love and poor Demeter watched helplessly as the days told the story of their love.

Osephus life had been made so much easier for all of this. So grateful was he one day, that he felt he needed to share it. He went to the Oracle's house, to the one old friend he knew would appreciate and share his excitement. She was out on her bench her little loves around her. Golden eyes lifted to meet Osephus own.

Before he could spill out his joy she spoke, "I found her, I found Sara. She eluded me for a while but I have found her." Osephus stopped, his mouth shut. Oh dear.

PART FIVE

We have all heard it, the whisper in the back.

In the corner of our thoughts and minds,

he whisper of what we lack.

Always around the edges, it calls from shores unknown

a lost piece of ourselves, perhaps, longing for home.

In the stillness of the day, in our early morning jog,

around the edges of our sunshine, deep within life's fog.

A thought within a thought, a memory we can't quite reach,

of a time we may remember or something we still seek.

But it's there, ever so small.

We hear the call,

of that thought.

Hades was getting dressed, not just dressed, but really dressed, as Osephus would say. Hades smiled at that thought. The vibration of love had brought joy back to the edges of his life.

Osephus was tidying Hades quarters, trying to muster the courage to tell him the whole story of Sara. How the Oracle had found her, well, who she is now at any rate. He had gone over the whole story in his head and it had sounded magnificent. What a hero he was in the narrative! Now if he could just make his mouth make words.

Hades with humming, Osephus stood up, all thoughts no longer occupying his neural pathways. Hades was happy. Osephus narrowed his eyes. What day was it? Festival of the Solstice. Lots of merriment and a god get together of sorts. That would not make Hades smile like that at all.

Mid Osephus thought Hades blurted out his intentions, "Today is the day I'm going to ask for Persephone's hand in marriage, she will be Queen of the Underworld." And Hades then hummed more of the song his heart was waltzing too.

Osephus was speechless. Now he was in a predicament. If he told Hades now, well, who knew how he would take to Sara not really being Sara but now being someone named Luece. This Luece person probably did not remember anything.

Osephus remembered who he had been because this was his first existence since falling to Earth. But he had fallen with others that had come back multiple times already. Some of them losing the thought of where they came from. Forgetting entirely of what magnificent beings they truly were. He reached for where his wings once spanned.

Closing his eyes as he remembered to sun on his face, the wind caressing his body. His sigh brought him back to the present moment of reality. Yes, better to just let Sara or Luece, to just be where she was, creating her own new life, while Hades was happy in his own. That would be the best.

His sigh of relief was audible enough Hades eyes turned towards him. Osephus stopped breathing at his attempt to not think of Sara. Ever so often he became suspicious that Hades could read thoughts.

Some of the gods and goddess and even some humans, had the gift of telepathy, and who knew what Hades could or could not do. Hades averted his eyes, Osephus regulated his breathing pattern quietly. Had Osephus, in that moment, spoke what he knew, spoke his truth, a great change would have altered history, stopping several wars and the blood bath that came after. But he did not own his truth, for courage is not so easily garnered in the dark.

They left for Mount Olympus, Hades radiating confidence, as he should. His proud, regal splendor, drawing attention wherever he went. The hall of Olympus was set with a banquet table in the middle.

The gods met four times a year to discuss their politics with the humans. In order to keep their places of power the humans had to believe in the gods, it gave them the energy and resources they needed to live longer lives while using supernatural gifts they had acquired through the millennia's.

These festivals were a means to be seen by the humans as well encouraging their continuation of beliefs. Osephus had marveled how little the humans accepted in return for their service, their worship. Poor Osephus could not see that his story ran quite perpendicular to theirs. Though for him, no one had handed the story down. He had just simply, one choice at a time, walked the path he was now on. Where as the humans handed stories from generation to generation, making the gods seem even more powerful than they did in the beginning.

Such festivities lasted for days and then the pain of sobriety lasted a few more days after the fun. Even the gods had their limits. Osephus had noticed Hades joy, yes, he would call it that. Though he hardly recognized it on Hades.

Hades and Persephone had exchanged glances the first day or two and by the third day if you saw one of them you saw the other. The mighty Hades, who could not get enough alcohol to quench the thirst of his addictions had found another addiction far more dangerous to his liver than his beloved alcohol. Hades had worked the whole plan out by the end of the Solstice, he was confident in himself.

Persephone loved him, he would, out of love and respect for her, do this right. He would go to Zeus, he could be a terrible creature but he felt his love for Persephone made him better. Almost like Sara. He caught himself. None of that today. This was far better. Persephone would choose to come with Hades, something Sara never did. Persephone's laugh carried over his thoughts and smothered the furrows on his forehead. His dark eyes lighting up once again at her voice.

At the end of the festival Hades found himself in front of Zeus. Something crept over Hades that he had not felt in so long it took a moment to understand what it was, fear. He had taken what he wanted or manipulated situations to get what he wanted without giving an account for it for so long, no one told him no because they were no longer given the opportunity to tell him no.

Demeter came and stood by Zeus. Hades reached for Cerberus's middle head. His hell hound was no match for Zeus but he could make Demeter limp. That brought a smile to Hades face. Zeus took that as a cue to ask what the mighty Hades would like, as that would be the only reason that he stood in Zeus's court.

"I would like the hands of Persephone." Hades dark eyes rose to meet the God of lightning.

Zeus stared hard. In the beginning, after the fall, he and Hades had been comrades and brothers. Creating the world they wanted and had envisioned before both had such a thirst for power. Comradeship could not continue to grow in such an environment.

They were known as a type of rival Ying and Yang. The God of the dark standing before the god of light. Demeter had made it to Zeus before Hades could. She was not blind to what had been going on over the Solstice. Her conversation with Persephone had yielded absolutely nothing. Persephone had set her heart and mind on Hades and there would be no turning that.

Her mistake was in underestimating Demeter. Zeus had doted on Persephone, she was truly his princess. Normally he would give in to everything related to Persephone and what she wanted. But he could not ignore what was going on in front of him and did not need Demeter to point out what he was already seeing.

Zeus was angry, very angry. Hades had taken so much, he would not take Zeus's light down to the dark depths of his kingdom. Zeus's eyes narrowed at that thought. Persephone was currently locked up. It was easy to feign his daughter was tired after the festivities and Hades would be gone before he let her out.

"No!" billowed from Zeus's chair. As Zeus jumped to his feet Hades stroking motions of Cerberus lessened, the tone of Zeus's voice indicated he may need both his hands and all of his wits. "You shall not have any part of my household. I have put up with you being near her in The Valley of the gods but no more, this ends now."

Many things flashed their Hades mind while he stood there, anger being a very dominant part of the experience. But he had seen some of the "lesser gods," as he called them, meander in. Cerberus could take Demeter, goddess of agriculture or not, Cerberus had never liked Demeter. Hades could at least be Zeus's equal but with the other beings in the room, well, Hades knew when it was time to withdraw.

68

Hades and his hell hound were sure to lose their spa membership in the Underworld if they were not careful.

Hades bowed his head in acknowledgment, only his eyes showing the depths of his emotions and they were so dark he would have to be within arms length to see. No one would want to be that close at said moment in time. He thanked his hosts for their graciousness and then he retreated, his anger vibrating around him like a damp fog. He had grown so presumptuous of his own strength that this blind sighted him.

When he arrived in the underworld Osephus greeted him joyfully, and for the first time in a long time Hades slapped him. Poor Osephus! Excited for his master's happiness which he was so sure of. This was more than a blow to him physically. It changed him. Sweet Osephus, never power hungry. The switch was flipped. He had of course no idea what Hades had just gone through. And Hades in his fear, anger and pain, would not tolerate joy. No words were exchanged once Osephus could breathe deeply and calmly again. He bowed and left the room.

Hades took up pacing, what to do? He knew Persephone loved him, he felt it. Such a woman! Such a goddess! Finally someone fitting, someone worthy to be called the Queen of the Underworld.

He smiled as he pictured her at the head of his banquet table. He was lost in thought for just a moment before he remembered why he was upset, what should he do? Then the thought crept through his mind, like a cat after a mouse, what if they eloped. He knew she loved him. He could take her from the Valley of the gods. This is what she wanted anyway, she would be excited at such a plan.

He would have to pick a day that Demeter was not with her. He would have Osephus ask Dahlia off handedly what Demeter was doing this week. Osephus was bright, he would figure out the details and he, Hades would then bring his Persephone at home!

For the rest of the day as well as the next few Hades was in high spirits. Osephus watched from the corner's. His grudge would fester throughout several lifetimes but for now in this lifetime he knew his limits and those limits were reduced to skulking in the corner in silence unless spoken directly to.

Hades of course never noticed. The Oracle, however, did, on the next visit that Hades paid her. She motioned for Osephus to stay with her after Hades was finished. She watched his body language as she told him where Sara/Luece was. Previous ecstasy over said matter was completely gone. Her brow furrowed, somewhere she was missing something, no matter, she had done her part now what Osephus did with that information was up to him.

Osephus graciously thanked her, she had written all the information down for him. After all, a happy Hades was really the best Hades for everyone concerned. As Osephus wandered back to the great hall in the underworld he shoved the paper deep into his pant pocket. Where once there was the desire to see his master succeed, sullen bitterness welled at the thought of him. He, Osephus, had given up much, including himself, to help Hades succeed.

Osephus had never asked for much, really anything, but never had he felt such a betrayal as this at such a level. Let him have his Persephone. Anyone could see the symbols on the wall for that outcome. He, Osephus, would keep his head down and mind to his own doings.

We often think that we have actions that we can create in a passive aggressive way that will actually change the other person's thinking. That's not usually how that works. The other person, most of the time, does not even notice our play at retaliation and we end up consuming our own time and energy to prove a point to someone that does not have the capacity or even the want to understand our behavior in the first place. Osephus went on for several days in said mindset before he came to his senses and realized what he was actually doing, but that is further into our story. I'm getting ahead of myself.

Hades met Osephus at the door entering his great hall. He explained his plan about Persephone and eloping, as well as Osephus's part in said plan. Hades never once looked at Osephus face or worried about a reply.

Osephus had long ago made his peace with his fate and Hades embraced that mindset, never thinking Osephus could or would change his mind about the path he first chose. When Hades was finished with his glorious plan he paused to breathe and finally looked Osephus. Osephus asked when his master would like said plan carried out.

The next day Osephus found himself on the path leading to The Valley of the gods to speak with Dahlia. The sun warmed him to his bones, it felt, and the same breeze that moved through the willows touched his cheeks. This part of his journey was truly the epic part. Not kidnapping the damsel who would be in distress after the kidnapping instead of before.

He was not as convinced as Hades that Persephone would be excited. The goddess was well known for her love of pomp and splendor, sneaking off into the sunset was not going to have the same effect as the blessing of Zeus would have. Dahlia was, thankfully, off in the stream. She was washing dirt off fruit she had gathered for her mistresses, her hair pulled back, brown tresses stuck here and there to the sweat on her forehead. Her dark eyes greeted Osephus with a question as she saw him draw him nearer.

He talked about the last Solstice, asking her how it was for her. She answered everything nicely. The wonder at the servant of Hades being here alone was not lost on her, she had heard Demeter and Zeus's lively discussion on the matter concerning Hades and

Persephone. She knew their opinion of Persephone becoming Queen of the Underworld.

She had also bore the blunt of having to listen to Persephone go on and on about how it should have been her choice, that she should not have been negated in the discussion. The same conversation Dahlia had endured for several days now, as it seemed that Persephone had it in a loop. Osephus was a bit of a relief, especially if Hades was not too far behind.

Hades had explicitly told Osephus that he was not to tell Dahlia what Hades was plotting. He knew the handmaiden would never risk the wrath of keeping such a secret from Demeter and it would be Demeter, not Zeus, that the poor individual would give an account to. Taking a risk for all of them.

Osephus had asked every polite question he could think of. How to ask what day Demeter would not be there, without asking the question, well, such cunning was usually Hades to enjoy and not Osephus strong point. Through his prattle Dahlia had loosened up her tongue a bit, she did enjoy visiting and the goddess did not ask her what she was doing or how she felt about things, besides, Osephus was not the handsome one for sure, but he was sweet and very attentive in a way that made Dahlia's eyes light up.

Through their conversation Osephus learned that Demeter was going to visit Aphrodite on the next phase of the moon. Persephone would then be with Dahlia alone by the river. Osephus visited with her until the sun started to go down and Demeter cried out for her. He kept out of sight of the goddesses. Best to not have any extra questions such as why was he there alone. Mainly he did not want to answer that specific question. Demeter could spot a lie with her eyes closed. Osephus had wondered if she could smell them.

On his walk home, back into the darkness of his life, he wandered for just a moment if he should not tell the truth to Hades about

Luece/ Sara. More now for his own wellbeing and lifespan, if Hades ever found out that Osephus had known and not told him, well, that would be the end of Osephus's unnaturally long life. Most likely a painful end, he shuddered, somehow he would slip it into the conversation when he returned, he thought to himself.

Hades met him at the door of his great room, he even opened it eagerly. He wanted to know everything. "Had Persephone asked about him? About his well being?" Osephus tried multiple times to interject between the volley of questions to share about Luece/Sara, and both times Hades became aggravated and agitated.

"I don't want to hear about anything other than what I sent you!" he bellowed, motioning for Osephus to take a seat.

Osephus told him that he'd only spoken to Dahlia, Hades nodded in approval. Nasty Demeter would then have the leg up on it all had Osephus not kept the information between he and Dahlia. He told Hades of when Demeter would be gone.

Hades jumped up, absolute joy on his face, something that had not been there in a very long time. "I will go and take her from my wife then, Persephone will be my Queen!"

Osephus did not think it pertinent to mention Luece at this time. After all, Hades was clearly in love. To be sure, who knew what Hades would have done with the information had Osephus given it to him.

We are all so funny in that way. Something we could never live without, something so dear we are in a constant state of fear that we may lose it ,well, time has a way of erasing the first taste of that pain after loss and we find we can live again, often better than before.

At any rate, we will never know what Hades would have done with the information because Osephus chose not to give him said information. We do know what he did beyond that moment. The great king of the Underworld patiently, lovingly, drunkenly, waited for Demeter to part. Where he then made his way to The Valley of the gods with Osephus in tow.

Osephus could not keep up and quite frankly he did not want to. He had a very bad feeling about this, the type of feeling that you know it was not something that you ate. But no one would be able to dissuade Hades from his path now.

Persephone was sitting on a blanket, Dahlia reading to her when the pair arrived. Persephone rose to greet Hades, her eyes afire with his boldness. She sent Dahlia off to gather flowers for the banquet room that Zeus kept full. Osephus happily trailed after Dahlia, wherein Persephone turned her full attention to Hades. What did the king of the Underworld want with her on such a lovely day? Her laugh echoed through The Valley when he told her.

Hades brow furrowed, a laugh was not what he had expected. He tried again to explain his plan, they would leave The Valley immediately having an exuberant wedding at he, Hades, glorious banquet hall, with all of the Underworld to see. She would be his Queen. And he sat back, his face glowing with excitement while he caught his breath after what he felt was an effective narrative of a happily ever after situation.

Persephone looked at him, this time with concern on her face. She had enjoyed her time with Hades, he fascinated her in ways that she had not known before. He made her laugh and that was no easy accomplishment, as the goddess of Spring had an everlasting air growth around her but not of mirth. Had Hades convinced Zeus Persephone would have been overjoyed with the outcome but she would not risk her status with her father nor the other gods and go against Zeus. Those were consequences that she would not face for anyone.

There was a deep silence that descended over The Valley after she told him. Osephus and Dahlia felt it where they sat. Osephus belly did that flip flop thing, the one that happened right before Hades released his anger on anyone nearby. Osephus had been thankful for this bit of gastro intestinal help on many occasions and had learned to accept the hard truth that it was usually right. He glanced towards what he hoped was the happy couple. No, they did not look like a happy couple.

Persephone had a settled look on her face as she studied the willows, while Hades looked like he may breath fire or burst into flames, combustion looked inevitable, at any rate. His dark eyes focused unbelievingly on Persephone's face.. He then did something Osephus never remembered hearing, he pleaded with Persephone.

This softened her, she honestly was fond of the king of the Underworld. The seed was planted and love very well could have grown. Love that Hades was so very hungry for. He had not forgotten, through the centuries, what that love felt like and he felt a pang as he saw her eyes turn and soften towards him.

She would not be moved, though, her pride was too strong for such a thing. And no matter how strong Hades thought he was, he was no match for Zeus and Demeter. She gathered her things and called for Dahlia, while kissing his cheek after her explanation.

Hades was very still. He remained still as Persephone and Dahlia left The Valley and Osephus crept up, terrified to breathe. Slowly Hades rose and made his way back to the Underworld. Osephus made not one sound. Stealth, was his intuition, to get calmly back to a place of safety. He knew there would be a reckoning after it all settled on his master.

Once again Luece flitted through his mind. How history would have been written so differently had Osephus had the courage in that moment to tell Hades what he knew. No one knew, though, better than he, what Hades was capable of doing in certain moods.

Osephus had no way to know how Hades would handle this long term. They were to the gates of the Underworld when Hades turned on his heel and faced Osephus, asking him if he had heard anything. Thank the other gods he had not heard but that little bit of dialogue that had wafted in on the breeze. Hades, the master of lies, could sniff a lie out. Whatever had happened between the two was safely between the two of them, Osephus assured him.

Hades turned around, appeased that his shame and rejection was known by no other than himself. His mind had been working through the whole scenario. He had replayed it, trying to fathom exactly what had happened.

Osephus asked to be excused and Hades waved him off without really listening, he was on round three of the replay and what tentatively could have been done differently. As he replayed it his anger dwindled. He was also drinking as he replayed it all, nothing like a good ale to help ones focus, he was on a pint of ale. So he felt his focusing was about to get keen.

He slammed down his cup, of course she was afraid of Zeus! Poor sweet Persephone. She obviously loved Hades, he thought, she simply had no choice in the matter. It was up to him, why it was his responsibility to help her, she was not Zeus's pet!

He slammed his fist down with emphasis, she was a free being. A goddess! And what a goddess she was... but what could he do to help her? How could he fear of such tyranny so that they could be together? Pint number two was enlisted to help sort the mess out. Of course! It came to him, blessed thinking ale, the Oracle! She would know!

It was well into the night by now. Of course Hades was not aware of the time at all, and even if he were, honestly he felt everyone in the Underworld lived to serve him, so the time most likely would not have been taken into consideration. He stood up his second wind of enthusiasm waving over his entire being, he swayed a bit. More ale than he thought inside of him, he had drank some more in celebration of his brilliance.

He would call Osephus, that would help. Osephus, groggy eyed and shuffling, came when called. Hades explained to him that they should be off shortly to see the Oracle and that Osephus would have to definitely assist him as the ale was stronger than what he remembered.

Osephus thought, very briefly, of making Hades aware that it was now the middle of the night and the Oracle would be fast asleep. But it was a very brief thought due to years of twenty four hours a day service. Hades stumbled a bit but made his way with Osephus support to the Oracle's house.

Normally Osephus would have made it there first and given the oracle time to adjust but Hades needed Osephus for actual physical support to walk. Hades beat on the door with all of his might, muttering how people should be dependable at all times of the day. Osephus turned his face to roll his dark eyes.

The Oracle awakened, startled by the banging. She hurried though, knowing only the king of the Underworld would have her be awake at such an hour. Her golden eyes pierced directly into Hades dark eyes as she opened the door. It was the most reproach he would receive from her but Osephus shivered a wee bit from the feeling that it emitted. He believed her glare was the foundation for "if looks could kill." Hers at the very least should be able to wound. She ushered them in, politely taking in the fact that Hades was leaning heavily on Osephus.

"To what do I owe the pleasure of such a visit," she asked, her eyes still penetrating Hades soul.

All the ale had made its way to the neurons in Hades brain, causing a good amount of difficulty for said neurons to fire in the correct sequence. Yes, he was drunk. Osephus was impressed. Hades was no lightweight. Persephone was some goddess for sure.

Osephus made sure that he looked everywhere but at the Oracle, realizing that she would and probably did know, that he had not given Hades the information on Luece. He took this opportunity to prompt Hades on why they were there. Surprisingly Hades told them everything. Though the two knew that Hades being vulnerable now was due to his friendship with ale and that both would kindly forget the whole story later.

"How do I rescue her from Zeus and liberate her? How do I free the woman I love so that she can take her rightful place at my side?" He sat heavily down beside one of her pets.

It was Kye, and he slunk away, he did not appreciate the smell of his mistresses companion, and it made his tails twitch. He did not care if Hades loved him or not. He was grateful that he had not brought Cerberus with him, filthy hellhound, smelled like death and lost hope.

The Oracle looked to Osephus once more, trying to derive from someone what was really going on. She knew Hades high esteem of himself was not shared by many and that Hades simply chose to believe everyone saw him the way that he saw himself. Magnificent, and a rare specimen of a god.

She had heard from the spirits of the daughter of Zeus and Demeter, knew that the goddess was a beautiful goddess and looking for a suitable match. Word of Hades meeting with Zeus at the hall of the gods had also reached her. She knew that Zeus did not approve. So from those thoughts, and a few more drunk sentences, she pieced most of the truth together. She knew Persephone would not go against Zeus, at least not willingly.

A sigh from her soul escaped her lips. She had one master. It did not matter her beliefs or her thoughts, her journey had led her to this moment with Hades.

She got them both something to drink. She put a few herbs extra in Hades to help sober him up. She did not want to have to repeat all of this at a time he would want to remember details. While they sipped their drinks she went to her divination room and asked the spirit guys what she should do.

Casting her Runes with a heavy heart, she set her intention for clarity. As her runes fell over the cloth, she released her animosity. After all this was Hades journeys not hers. Despite how Hades was today she remembered him as Samiel. She had loved Samiel dearly, that love still trickling to the being that was in her home, bearing very little resemblance to the Samiel she knew. She would do what she could to lead him back to love, perhaps that would help him remember who he truly was.

The runes led her to a scroll that she had on binding. Now why would the guides lead her to a binding spell when she was trying to work out how to liberate Persephone? Her brow narrowed in thought as she lay her runes down again for clarity. She did not need liberation it seemed, because Hades had deceived himself so well in thinking he knew the answer to be anything other than what it truly was.

She shuddered at the implications that this brought to the table. At one time her hands were not so tied by fear. Many were the nights a fortunate soul escaped because the Oracle worked her own form of liberating magic from the mess that Hades created and his incessant need for power. She knew it all stemmed from his fears and those fears had sprouted tiny fears of their own until the drinking and the growth of power were the only thing that Hades felt. Her resilience for his antics had slowly dwindled through the years, she did not have the stamina to resist him as she once did.

So, against her own truth, she read the scroll that her faithful guides led her to through the reading of her runes. The scroll spoke of the magic that was held in a simple pomegranate seed. How it represents regeneration, life, and look at that, marriage. It being a symbol of the indissolubility of marriage.

The gods were funny like that, in the way that they held such superstition in high regards. Their power in lifestyle causing their actual perception of the reality in the moment to wane. Making it very easy for something to become real simply through the effort of their belief that they put into it. Hades only had to get Persephone to eat 4 pomegranate seeds, one for each celebration of Solstice, and she would be bound to him until death do they part.

She put away the scrolls and thanked her guides for their wisdom. With conflicting emotions of her role in what she felt was going to be a terrible decision, she told Hades and Osephus everything she learned up to this point.

Hades was sober and his excitement radiated from his very being. He jumped up, lifted her, and swung her around. She regained her balance a little after he set her down. He was rather large, she not so much at all. As she was only four foot eleven inches tall. Her spinning head and sore bones made her feel like a doll in the god's arms.

"Osephus, find me pomegranate seeds as soon as now!" Hades bellowed.

Osephus patted Kye on his love spot, being careful not to hit his murder spot. Oh yes, he hit that by accident one day. Charming creatures until you hit the murder spot.

Osephus jumped to his feet, nodded at the Oracle, and sped off. Hades went back to his room leaving the Oracle to clean up. She found a few runes off to the side of where she had done her reading.

How had she missed that? She went back to the scrolls that she had been directed to. There, if Persephone did not eat all four pomegranate seeds she would only be bound for the portion of the year of the number that she ate.

This made the Oracle feel better. Bless the guides, keeping their small secrets to save some chaos. No sense in using chaos all up at once, after all there would be no creation without chaos. It was best to spread such large amounts out, and Hades was walking chaos, for certain. As she crawled into her bed with her pets, she felt a sense of relief. The universe would help Persephone figure this out before she became another Hades passing addictions.

PART SIX

"What is your perception?" fairy godmother asked one day.

"You have to know what you want so that we may find a way.

In order to create the reality that you love

you must know your desires, the parts that they are made of.

You must feel you are magnificent, know without a doubt

the essence of who you are and what you are about."

I have been told that certain cultures do not let their members read great books of knowledge until they are over forty. This is based off the theory that they do not have the self realization to perceive what they believe based on there environment, versus what they are reading, thereby missing the spiritual truth in front of their eyes. Hades was well over forty when he fell to Earth.

His age: timeless, as he became a god. When he first fell his perception was clear of what he wanted to create but after so many centuries of thirsting for power and creating from the fear of losing that power his perception of the reality around him was misshapen and misinformed. This made him more dangerous than ever.

Ospehus was pondering this when he should have been sleeping. Instead he was wide awake, looking for seeds as there were none to be found in the Underworld, so he had made his trek to the world of men, where they also were sleeping. He was not about to be abused by anyone other than Hades. He knew Hades well enough that as long as he came home with the seeds all would be well. So he slumped under a tree and slept until the morning rays of the sun woke him up.

He jumped, The rays were warmer than they should be and he had slept longer than he should have. He rushed to the market, finding pomegranate seeds to be more difficult to find than he had imagined.

The sun was going down in the sky when he had located a total of three pomegranate seeds. He remembered that the Oracle had said four, but she had not really said why she needed four. Perhaps that was just her favorite number.

Osephus felt that three would be fine, especially since that was all that there was to be found. He was correct, when he arrived back at the great hall Hades only recognized the fact that he had pomegranate seeds, obviously he had not heard a specific number and nothing was discussed as to why it took Osephus so long to find them. Osephus shifted from one foot to the other as he handed the seeds to Hades, to state it simply, he had a bad feeling about all of this.

Hades did not notice the mood in the room but excitedly, once again, tasked Osephus with finding out when Demeter would be elsewhere and when Persephone would be alone in The Valley of the gods. That meant that he would get to see Dahlia once again. That was fine by him he thought, and a smile passed his lips.

He found Dahlia, she told him that Demeter would be gone the next week. Osephus took his time visiting her, telling Hades later that it took him awhile to find her. They made plans to leave for the Valley of the Gods the day that Demeter would first be gone.

It was warm outside, the air smelt of the blooms that were ornamenting everything around them as they made their way to The Valley of the gods. Hades was difficult to keep up with, especially since Osephus had to carry the basket of food. Hades had a meal prepared and was planning on using the pomegranate seeds as an appetizer. Might as well get the best over with first. He felt that a meal would be an excellent offering of peace for his heart's desire considering how they had last parted.

Osephus felt there must be a whole pig in the basket as he was practically dragging it behind him. The humans made so many sacrifices a year and Hades would be little their need for acceptance.. Well here they were, offering their own fatted calf for acceptance. If he had not wanted to eat with

Dahlia later he would just say that out loud. All this work made him feel like he could tackle anything. As he dragged the basket it was tempting to make some snide remark, but it was best to just wipe the sweat away, he thought.

Persephone looked up, her brows furrowing in a scowl over her dark eyes, for just a moment. She caught herself and managed a smile.

As stated earlier in our story, Persephone was attracted to Hades, she admired him greatly, but she was no fool to cross her parents over this matter.

She had given it much thought since their last encounter, and had decided that even had Zeus approved, Queen of the underworld was not a good fit. She was, after all, goddess of agriculture, and though Hades saw lost souls as cattle, that was not the cattle that she governed. She was still the daughter of Demeter, though, and as such she would be cordial to the King of the underworld.

Persephone rose and greeted him cordially, which added to the already false perception that he had. He gestured at the basket that Osephus was still dragging behind himself, sweat pouring down Osephus face, asking if she would like to eat lunch with him. She nodded her approval and motioned for Dahlia to come help Osephus set it up.

The two servants took their small portion and made themselves happily scarce as their master and mistress would be occupied for a time. Osephus, still raw over carrying the basket so far, took pride in that he did not need pomegranate seeds to woo Dahlia. He stood up straighter, puffing out his chest as he thought of his manhood in comparison to Hades.

This was quickly subdued by the slight fear that Hades could read his mind. He did not know for certain that Hades could read minds, but it did seem as much at times. He shivered and hurried Dahlia on, trying to think of something else. Dahlia turned, smiling at him. That changed his thoughts. A happy sigh slipped from his lips as his dark eyes danced with a light that had been long dormant.

Persephone let Hades fill her plate. They spoke of world matters, how it felt that the humans love and worship was not what it once was. Persephone commented on a possible pestilence to increase prayer and morality, while hades eyes roamed between Persephone's lovely mouth and the pomegranate seeds.

She had eaten one and was finishing the second when she noticed the look on Hades face. It was what world dominion looked like, she was sure of it. Such excitement on the brow while the lips were pursed in an "almost there" way.

She did not finish her plate, but asked Hades what he was really there for. So he told her, he told her everything, bearing his heart of how he knew she wanted to be with him as badly as he wanted to be with her, knowing it was only the matter of her parents, standing in the way. He divulged the tail of the pomegranate seeds. Her face changed throughout the narrative of his story from polite listening to horror. That set her on her feet.

"What have you done?" she cried out in anger, Hades was stunned by her response, he had been sure of her affection.

Persephone explained that she was fond of him but marriage! Without even asking! He had tricked her!

She was devastated and still very angry, Hades felt it was mainly the shock of it all. He knew she would come around once she had time to process the whole situation. Persephone was definitely processing but not in the light of Hades favor.

She was already trying to figure out how to fix this. Her father would help surely.. she was not positive of that though. He would be angry that she allowed herself to be so taken. As I previously mentioned the gods were very superstitious the older they became. They were at several centuries old so the paranoia had time to fester and grow. Her mind wandered more for a solution. Her mother! Demeter would stand with her in this.

Persephone knew by the love struck look on Hades' face that she was going to have to handle this correctly in this moment or it would go badly quickly. She smiled at him, offering her hand, he greedily took it.

That did make her heart flutter, especially the look as his dark eyes met her. She felt it in the pit of her being. She quickly explained to him that especially since nothing could be done to reverse the process (she had thought of vomiting up the pomegranate seeds) that she would like to plan the wedding with her mother and close friends.

She looked up at him one more time, the lust obvious on his face. She was better than a good ale to him he felt.. The epitome of his reign of power, he saw no reason to deny her of her request, after all she was bound to him now. He called for Osephus, who had a much less awkward day, and after all that they brought was gathered they parted ways, with Hades promised whispers to be back tomorrow.

Persephone cried the whole way home. Dahlia had no idea what was going on. Osephus was fond of Dahlia but he would not risk the confidence of Hades for fondness.

Persephone had decided Demeter would be the best first line of defense . She rushed to her mother's quarters and between heart wrenching sobs told her all that happened. Demeter shot up out of her reclining sofa, so angry she paced for a moment. She was beyond angry at Hades but also at Persephone.

She railed at her daughter, the goddess asking repeatedly what was she thinking even entertaining the god of the Underworld and then she cried with her because she realized the likelihood of them getting out of the marriage was very little.

She asked her exactly how many pomegranate seed she had eaten. She would go to her Oracle and see what could be done then she would take the whole situation to Zeus. Honestly unsure of how he would react to it all.

In many ways Zeus had less compassion than even Hades. As mentioned previously when they had all first fallen they had great plans of sharing equal power. They were to be creators on an exponential level, but power is such a drug. Pushing you forward while sedating you in the little places in your soul that bring you true joy. Making you think having such power will have so much joy in the first place. But only robbing you of that joy as you sacrifice your values for the power you covet. Hades as well as Zeus did not know that joy is a special power, one that is a choice and cannot be taken by the larger man.

Demeter's Oracle lived in Mount Olympus. She was the Oracle for all of the gods. This caused her to live a very busy life.

Hades Oracle had adapted to the darkness of the Underworld, creating her own light and only answering to the likes of Hades. And though Demeter's Oracle lived in the light of mountain Olympus, the burden she carried from so many caused her to be blind to the brilliance around her. She was often curt because of this.

As oracles were not easy to come by the gods ignored her curtness, as long as she kept giving them wise counsel. Demeter rushed in, unannounced, spewing out everything that had just occurred. In her fear demanding an immediate answer. This Oracle was as white as parchment, so you could never tell when the blood was draining from her face. Her slate blue eyes peered from under her snow white hair, she was ageless.

The lack of amusement flooded across her face as she bowed to Demeter and went to gather her supplies. She asked Demeter exactly how many pomegranate seeds that Persephone had eaten. Demeter told her while pacing the floor, alternating between depression and anger. She had managed to avoid the very fate that her precious daughter was walking into. They were both goddesses of agriculture, it would be a slow, sure death for her darling child to live in such darkness.

"Hurry! Can't you see the mess we are in!"

The Oracle sighed, blowing her white hair out of her face. She explained to Demeter that thankfully Persephone had only eaten one and a half which would be likened to a third of the year. What was done was unbinding, Persephone was betrothed to Hades and bound to him but only for a third of the year. Demeter sprang up, that was the hope that she needed to propel her forward.

She knew Hades would not wait long to claim his bride, pompous god that he was, so her next destination would be Zeus, after she prepared herself of course. Demeter was very beautiful, she would have to be to catch the eye of Zeus. Her hair was the color of an acorn and eyes like the Atlantic after a storm, bringing hope to whoever they looked on.

She changed and freshened quickly, afterwards going to find Zeus. He had been planning a tour of the countryside and was in his chambers preparing. He liked to periodically walk among humans feeling that it added to their adoration of him performing small miracles, Demeter called them parlor tricks, as he went to the different villages. And they loved him deeply.

His blue eyes met Demeter's as she came in after Zeus's servant announced her, his dark brown curly hair hanging from his shoulders, his smile genuine. Demeter was very grateful that he was in such a good humor at the moment. May he keep it, passed through her thoughts. They talked about his route and the goals he had set.

He rambled on in his excitement and then looked, really looked at her. "What has the lovely Demeter really come to see me about? Your visits are always welcome but you do not usually come at such a time of day."

So Demeter told him everything, perhaps narrating more in Persephone's favor to make the god of the sky pity his daughter and feel wrath towards his brother Hades. It worked. Zeus's eyes deepened as he stood up. What was the meaning of such an act against him! How dare Hades cross such a line, especially with his daughter.

Demeter went on to tell him what her Oracle had said. Persephone would have to marry but would only have to spend one third of the year with Hades.

"One third!" he bellowed "is too much!"

He though, like the other gods, was a believer in the superstitious ways of the humans that they walked among. He would have to be content with one third. Once again proving that power, even a gods power, is given away easily if they have lost the gift of free thought.

Demeter cried on his shoulder and he held her in a moment of tenderness. After all, this was their beautiful Persephone. Zeus knew that he need not worry about seeking Hades for the conversation that would have to follow. Once Hades could not find Persephone for a space of time in The Valley of the gods, he would come to them, most likely gloating. Zeus snorted, his pride wounded at the ridiculousness that his daughter put him through. Demeter was not one to ignore or take lightly, he loved her, if nothing else he would sort this all out for her.

Zeus was not wrong nor did he have long to wait before Hades made his appearance, coming to claim his bride. Zeus was waiting in the great room in Olympus, it was a massive room full of pillars of marble. Large thrones were positioned in a circular manner around the room for when the gods met.

Zeus was at the head of the room where he resided during their festivals and meetings. He sat there now, staff in hand, braced for the events that were about to take place. They exchanged cordialities, discussing the state of affairs with the humans. They even set some goals of collaboration for some upcoming festivals.

Then Hades faced sobered up and he shared why he was there, telling Zeus of he and Persephone's great love and need to be together, of their passionate betrothal. This was finished with a smirk on Hades handsome face it, had been at least a century since he had best of Zeus. To know he bested him with his own daughter, the victory was just too sweet.

Zeus's face never changed, calmly he explained to the king of the Underworld that he had left out some very important details in his planning. Zeus went on to say that because Persephone had only eaten one third of the portion needed for a year she was only required to stay with Hades one third of the year, the other two thirds would be in her own kingdom of light.

Here his slate blue eyes sharpened as they bore into Hades dark eyes. Hades felt the pit of his stomach burn, he glanced at Osephus, it was not a look of appreciation It obvious and who he blamed for this very real problem. There was nothing Hades could do, he straightened himself up, sure that Persephone would choose to stay with him the whole year. Why wouldn't she want to be Queen of the Underworld all of the time, especially with the feelings that they had for each other.

Zeus told him to come back in two weeks time and they would have the wedding. When Hades insisted on seeing Persephone, Zeus stood, slamming his staff to the ground, energy vibrating around him.

"You have wielded these happenings to your own desires enough, we will take it from here!" the glint in his blue eyes as they snapped, well Hades had seen that look on his old friend's face before, it was never the prelude to a party.

Hades bowed as he rose from his chair, he would be back in two weeks, ready for his bride as well as the wedding, to claim what was his. Osephus, for lack of a better word, was abused all the way back to the underworld, wherein Hades made a trip to the Oracle's hut. In his anger, humiliation and frustration, tearing apart her room of herbs.

She clung to her three pets, hiding in a safe space under her house built for such a day as this, she connected daily to her guides and they had warned her that morning of what may take place. She had spent most of her day preparing. No man, or god per say, can control what Hades had pent up inside of himself, never letting it out wholly but playing a constant tug of war within himself with his dark and light. He wore himself out in the Oracles sacred space, trying to cause her the same hurt and humiliation that he felt, believing her to be the cause of him being the underdog once again. It was, of course, never his fault.

Hades left the oracles herbs, tinctures and her means of divination, broken and in disarray around her sanctuary. She climbed out of her hiding spot. She had heard Hades tell Osephus to find her.

She could see Osephus through the cracks of her nook, his face swollen, unrecognizable. His heart broken in places he thought better guarded. Osephus would not put his friend through the same fate that he endured.

He knew with the wedding so close if he could stall for a few days the Oracle would be safe. He ached for her broken things all around. She loved her plants and herbs almost as much as her strange pets. A lesser being her pets could have protected her from, but they were no match for Hades, he was too powerful for her magical darlings and she would not risk their safety.

She held them to her and cried, sobs from the pit of her being wracked her body. For all that she could create and divine, she could not create and divine her own freedom. She had helped many a soul escape the darkness of the underworld through the centuries. She would not easily forgive Hades for this, but she was smart enough to stay hidden until Persephone arrived. That would take Hades mind off of his wounded pride. Poor goddess, she had no idea of the life she would be walking into, her being accustomed to light.

The Oracle had not seen Hades so smitten as he was now. She had known him before the fall, as previously stated, but that was a different love. Osephus was one of the few that called Hades a friend from before.

She clicked her tongue, lot of good that did Osephus from the look of him now. Osephus had told her stories of Hades as Samiel with Sara as well as their great love for each other. She saw no remnant of that angel in the visage that had tore her beloved home apart. Who most certainly would have done damage to her physically had he found her. She shuddered, shaking the feeling off as she cleaned up. The goddess most certainly could not get here fast enough.

Two weeks passed, an extremely long two weeks for the inhabitants of the underworld. Osephus received no more beatings but this was more from the fact that Hades did not want him to be

bruised for the wedding festivities. The mental torture, however, was kept in full dispatch on a regular feeding schedule.

If Osephus could have sped up time he most assuredly would have. The thought of Dahlia coming with her mistress was a happy thought to him, a beacon of light while he waded through the torrent of emotions that Hades unleashed on him. Dahlia would be sent ahead to the underworld while Hades and Persephone toured the countryside amongst the humans after their wedding.

There would be a selection of the most powerful humans at the wedding, but in order to appease the common people , the actual people that lined the gods and goddesses pockets, they would go from village to city after the wedding to the festivals in their honor. Their had not been a wedding amongst the gods in several decades , this one was promising to be a massive event as the goddess of agriculture was worshipped and loved all over, and Hades, well, he was feared all over. Being a consistent emotion related to him, at least.

Persephone had spent her two weeks in an array of emotions. Her parents had been very upset with her, she knew it was her mother's love that kept the wrath of Zeus from consuming her and her lack of aptitude for what had been presented to her. She had berated herself off and on, especially while she planned the wedding and all that went with it with her mother.

Her emotions varied from horror to excitement. After all excitement is often one flick away from fear. Many times we cannot tell the first from the second, jumping to the assumption of fear because we do not take the time to understand ourselves. As we get older we realize that fear is OK, without it we would never have courage. Persephone was needing large amounts of that courage.

She was sitting in her study brushing her long black hair out while her incense burned in front of her. Tomorrow was the day, her day of reckoning. But then... what would it be like to be Queen of the Underworld?

This was where her mind flicked her fear into excitement. She envisioned her throne full of flowers all around. Her adoring layman grateful for her beauty. This pepped her up considerably, envisioning the music and the atmosphere.

Sure it was difficult to envision all of this, especially since she herself had never actually been to the Underworld. Demeter had though, and she had incredible stories to tell. So as the goddess lay her head on her pillow she felt satisfaction in two areas, Hades was not ugly and she would be a Queen. The rest would work itself out. After weeks of struggle within herself this was a good night to feel relief.

The morning of the wedding had the Underworld in as much of an uproar as the world above. Hades was in top spirits but all of the servants knew on such a day as this one should dot their I's and cross their t's. It had been whispered among the servants that Persephone was good and kind, Osephus telling them all of his interactions. This had created a spirit of hope.

Centuries with Hades had weathered the best of them so the goddess of agriculture was something to be excited about. They had taken great detail in her quarters. Osephus had seen to Dahlias, to make it warm and inviting. Even the Oracle had donated trinkets for Persephone's room. Protections, she called it, as she muttered how she wished she could protect her from Hades.

There was a small entourage going to the wedding to help carry things back and the other half would go along for the honeymoon that would be spent amongst the humans in various towns and villages. They were taking several wagons just for this purpose, as there would be a massive amount of gifts and offerings. Hades looked handsome, even the Oracle admitted that to herself as she hurried past him.

Osephus could see flickers of his old friend in Hades that day. He saw Samiel. His heart squeezed with grief when he thought of Sara. A small portion of him felt like he was betraying her. He shook himself, best to pay attention to the present moment and keep Hades in his good spirits. Osephus had pushed out of his mind what may happen when Persephone went home after three months. Best to not dwell on it, they would know soon enough.

The wedding was massive, there had not been a wedding between the gods in so long that all of the gods, demigods and anyone that had a smidge of a god in them, they came. As well as a few humans that were chosen for the role they played in beefing up the human's worship and adoration of said God's. For the gods lived off of the power of belief and through this grew their strength. There were so many willing humans, ready to hand their own power away to be validated by something they felt greater than themselves. Zeus had enough feet food to feed the world, Osephus thought, as he gazed at all the preparations while overseeing the unpacking of what they brought.

Because this is a story of Hades and the morning star, we will not go into great detail or depths of the wedding. For great detail it would take to describe such a festivity. Despite Persephone's inner battle the weeks before the wedding ,no one would have ever known by her face, certainly not by the way she carried herself.

She did not wear white. She wore green, the color of the new buds on a fruit tree in Spring. Her dark hair wrapped in magnificent coils upon her head as a crown with flowers interwoven. The goddess of agriculture looked like the Earth she tended with a beauty and grace that had never echoed from those walls before that moment.

Hades dressed in black, fitting for his throne he felt , balancing his bride of light. The light from his eyes shown, as he gazed at Persephone, illuminating parts of his facial features long ago forgotten. In that moment the God of the Underworld felt joy. Something that his addictive personality did not walk with as the want for more was always on the edge of his brain. As he watched Persephone throughout the day he did not see how there could be any more than this to his life.

Osephus watched in awe as his master had only a small amount of alcohol. Hades did not want to numb his senses today, he wanted to feel all of this, all of her. She became his new beautiful addiction.

Persephone felt his gaze throughout the day, she would catch it and smile, her heart warmed by his adoration. Zeus, however, had known Hades for long enough to have a nagging wonder in his mind when would the sobriety of this hit Hades and what waves would that possibly create in Zeus's world?

Demeter was heartbroken. The victory of keeping her daughter two thirds of the year paled when she thought of her leaving on the morrow. The festivities kept her mind somewhat busy but not enough for her to worry to ease entirely. The wedding was of such a variety that the world remembered it for centuries to come.. To this day one does not think of Hades without remembering and possibly feeling sorry for the lovely Persephone .

It was dawn, god's, goddesses, humans and other such things were draped all over the hall of the gods, having enjoyed themselves until they fell were they stood. Demeter was seeing her daughter off. Zeus was nowhere to be found, he had all of Hades' love that he could stomach for the decade, he felt. Better to deal with Demeter's emotions all at once. Demeter did not look as if she had been up for days, fresh as the spring she loved even though it was the harvest season. She looked at Hades as she kissed her daughter goodbye.

Her eyes did not move from his face as she said, "I will see you in three months time."

Hades returned her gaze. He did not flinch. So in love was he that he had no doubt that Persephone would never choose to leave him, especially when she realized, really felt, what a spectacular role being his wife, the Queen of the Underworld, would be.

They left, bound for the city of Athens for a week of mirth and celebration and honor of their wedding. From there they would travel to Thebes, Delphi and Corinth for the same such occasion, spending a month of their honeymoon with the humans that worshiped them. Hades was so enamored by Persephone he noticed nothing else on the ride. Once again she felt his gaze on her face and grew warm with the knowledge of his admiration, the realization of how he wanted to touch her.

He had held her hand, lingering at the last stop as he had helped her to her seat. In his touch she felt a reckless passion, passion that he was so known for, she wondered warmly what this would mean for her once they were alone. A feat that on such a journey is not easy.

Every stop, every village, was full of drinking, eating and music with very little sleep. Hades so felt for Persephone that he would not rush this. That was for other women, not for the lovely Persephone. He would love her until she wanted him in a way that she could not do without him.

The king of the Underworld was not without charm, especially when charm was what he had the most time for. He did not make an advance on her the whole time that they celebrated across the countryside except to hold her hand as support or brush her shoulders as he laid a scarf over them. This was very effective, she felt his passion and restraint in the brush of his fingertips, in his gaze that met hers across the room. It was far more effective than anything else would have been. Hades had learned throughout his reign, as well as while he gained power, that patience, especially applied at just the right moments in life, yielded extraordinary results.

The day came when their travels of wedding festivities were over, they stood at the gates of the Underworld. Mortal man could not see said gates unless it was his time to pass through. Once in a while a mortal would stumble through unbeknownst to himself, much to his horror once he realized, as there was no way back through for said mortal.

Hades paused and turned to Persephone, smiling "Welcome home my Queen."

His tone of voice, hid dark eyes with his sharp features, she felt a flutter in the pit of her stomach. Not a desperate flutter, but one of excitement and desire. Desire that had a month to build inside of her. She took his hand, holding it with hers, gracing him with a genuine look of want with need in her own dark eyes. He felt his heartbeat faster, and what felt like tingling. Was he tingling? He was, all over his body. This was new and delightful.

The gates of his kingdom were massive, fifty feet tall and thirty feet wide. Made of marble, wood and stone, inscribed with enochian, the language of the angels. Impressive to the gods, terrifying to the souls who passed through it.

They were the delight of Osephus who had created the plans for them during the time that Hades still saw him as an equal, as they were building the life they felt was worth falling for. Said Osephus was waiting happily for the wedding party. He had been sent to the Underworld right after the wedding with Dahlia.

They were to get Persephone's chambers ready as well as the Underworld itself for the arrival of its new Queen. In that space of time they had formed their own, very happy, commitment to each other, careful to keep it to themselves. The gods were not overly fond of others stealing their moments, in fact they made it a habit to keep that from happening.

Hades felt that Osephus reaction of joy was because he, Hades was home, his ego aided Osephus in that moment in time. It never crossed his mind that Osephus may be happy over something else. He smiled back at Osephus, this was new and disturbing to Osephus but he brushed it off.

There was drinking and festivities late into the night, but Hades, as well Persephone's eyes, rarely wandered away from each other. As the night lengthened and grew to an end, their excitement of being alone in their own quarters overtook them. Hades stood, with Persephone's eyes on him, graciously thanked everyone and dismissed them for the evening, which was the morning by that time. Finally, he took his bride and consummated the marriage that he had wanted so very badly. So in love were they that the consummation lasted several days before Hades resumed his role of king of the damned, with his Queen by his side.

PART SEVEN

There are moments in our lives that resemble the seasons for us all,

our spring turns to summer, our summer turns to fall.

We miss the song of the bird in the spring as it turns,

we miss the sun from the summer as fall fires burn.

We forget to live in the moment, to delve in the now,

grieving for what was, never to allow,

the moment, the season, to rest in our soul.

We cling to the experience of echoes, or the next one, to behold.

Not for one moment did Hades ever entertain the thought that Persephone would go back to mount Olympus, they were so in love. Hades watched as the Underworld itself fell in love with Persephone. How could they not?

For the first time since he became king of the Underworld he did not mind sharing power, sharing anything, so long as it was with her. When he thought of her it was as if his body could not help the somatic response of smiling. So when the winter was over and her four months were done it was a definite shock to Hades system when she announced it was time to go home.

They had just finished the evening meal and were in the great room sitting about the fire. Osephus and Dahlia were exchanging subtle glances. Persephone had not been blind to what was forming before her but she had a kindness in her soul and would not stop what she saw, she also would not draw attention to it either.

The room seemed colder after Persephone's announcement to everyone that was in it. They had the most glorious four months that Osephus could remember, even before he fell he did not remember Hades in such a glorious state of mind. He felt a cold fear grip his heart not just for the repercussions that he would face as the scapegoat, but Dahlia, she would leave. His heart sank, he loved her and took ever opportunity to show her this. Spring had bloomed all through winter for Osephus that year and his soul he grew nauseous at the thought of spring being over so quickly.

Hades had not had an outburst of temper since before the wedding. Osephus thought of Persephone as the goddess of all for accomplishing this, not just the goddess of agriculture. The tension was growing with the silence.

While Persephone's gaze did not leave Hades face she explained that she loved him, she was happy with him, and Hades winced, but she was the goddess of growth. She could not stay in the darkness of the Underworld, she would whither away if she could not feel the warmth of spring, the sun in the showers. Hades sat speechless.

She tried to tenderly explain to him that it was nothing personal about him but everything to do with her. He was in no way prepared for this as he had simply expected her to want to stay with him. He had felt positive that their love would make up for the losses she felt since leaving Olympus. Though he loved her he still had a problem with the concept that others had needs and they were not the same as his.

He rose, his eyes hardening, betrayal stirring in his heart. He bowed to her and went to his chambers. He slammed his door and paced for a bit. Walking over to where he kept his alcohol he picked up a bottle. It felt as though he had been kicked in the gut.

The last few months he had not really drank at all. Persephone being near him was intoxicating. Sure, he had drank socially, but not to the excessiveness that he was known for. He had not felt this good in centuries, this love that they had for each other, it flowed through his veins, creating something that he had not felt in his thirst for power, something that he had not felt since he had left Sara.

His hand paused with the bottle in mid air. Sara. The pain washed over him again as the memory of the look on Sara's face came to the forefront of his mind. The memory of the day that he told her he chose to fall, the betrayal he felt then when Sara would not go with him.

There's had been a different connection than what he felt with Persephone, they could feel each other's pain. The first two centuries without Sara were unbearable, driving his need and want for power, pushing him to excel just in case she came home to him.. He felt something splash on his hand. Hades, king of the Underworld, he was crying.

106

He threw the bottle across the room, smashing it on the wall, picking up another and another until there were no glass objects left or alcohol or tears. He fell, crumpled, into his bed, summoning sleep as he felt once more the darkness creep over his soul like the fogs over the sea of death. Only there was no ferry man to carry him over this body of emotional water.

In the morning Persephone was packed, ready and waiting. She was leaving Dahlia to see over her affairs and belongings. This was really more for Dahlia and Osephus sake as she could not bear to see that look on their face again as when she had originally stated that she would be leaving.

She had thought that Hades would come to her chambers last night, she had grown to love him and her soul craved his touch on the last night that she would be there. Persephone, being the goddess of growth, knew in her heart that we must first love and attend to ourselves before we can love and attend to others.

She, too, harbored feelings of the betrayal she felt inside of herself about the way that Hades had tricked her into marrying him. He could not expect something as meaningful as what Demeter and Zeus had to come out of their communion after the origin of their reality. Yes, that betrayal still stung if she was honest with herself, and the goddess was still a goddess, harboring and holding feelings where she would harbor and hold feelings. It took her a century to forgive him for the way that he "asked" her to marry him.

She would miss Hades though, as well as her lovely friends she had made in the Underworld, but she missed the sunshine, air and rain on her skin more. The fog on the sea of death was not the fog that poured through The Valley of the gods on a new spring morning. Her heart beat with excitement when she thought of it and her face flooded with a smile as she hugged Dahlia and Osephus, winking at the latter.

Hades came to see her off and Persephone was surprised that she did not smell any alcohol on him at all. The truth was Hades was too depressed for even that but he would not show it to her, proud as he was. There was a moment when he felt like if he would just go to see her she would change her mind. She had to, he could not survive this pain of being left again, or tolerate the emotional pain of fear and rejection. But he never went, so he slept alone.

Osephus watched with slight concern as Hades wandered off. He could tell that the king was in deep thought and pain. Osephus, though chastising himself for it, felt compassion for Hades.

Osephus was full of joy, for the first time since Osephus had been breathed into existence by creator, he was in love. How grateful he was to Persephone for leaving Dahlia, out of the kindness of her heart. Had Persephone not been so kind, and because Osephus had such compassion for Hades, in that moment he would have been sorely tempted to tell Hades about Luece to help ease his pain. But he couldn't do that to Persephone, she was too kind. He sighed a happy sigh and came back to his senses, grateful to have Dahlia with him.

Persephone came back as fall was giving way to winter. Her normally pale skin almost as dark as her hair that was wrapped in coils on her head like the Queen she was. Hades was so delighted to see her. He was pale and thinner than when she had left as he had spent most of the time drinking in his chambers.

This had worked in Osephus favor. Hades had been so sullen and mopey that he either was swimming in his alcohol or asleep. Before the whole incident with the pomegranate seeds Osephus would have been inclined to coax Hades from his chambers, helping him to find some way to take his mind off of his pain. Hades, like the rest of us, would play a hell loop in his head. Everything was bad, he thought. Something would start out good, and then end bad. What was the point of existence? These "loops" of thought seemed to last longer and longer with Hades. The only way out was the end of the cycle.

Hades would get black out drunk at which point Osephus would find another addiction, taking Hades mind out of whatever "loop" it had fallen into. Osephus was, however, very happy with Dahlia, and with Hades drunk in his quarters, the two of them ran the underworld with their own love and dignity. They were running it as Hades and Persephone's representatives, of course, but Osephus made a point of calling Dahlia "my Queen" at every chance he had, enjoying the light that shone in her eyes from his banter.

So Hades met Persephone, pale, with butterflies mating in his stomach when he was near her. That's what they had to be doing by the feeling of it. Persephone had missed Hades. To be sure being top side was invigorating, the sunshine, the rain, the breeze on her face, all of it, really.

Zeus, though, had put her in her place rapidly, just because she was the queen of hell did not mean that she could overshadow his authority. He took pains to make sure that she recognized this reality. She felt the sting in this as she had never had any intentions of surpassing her father in the greatness that he felt he had achieved. She had enough of his blood in her to appreciate having the title of Queen of the Underworld added to her name, though the responsibility of lost souls even for a third of the year was heavy on her. The responsibility of ensuring crops and nature took a positive course was really enough.

Hades held her close, she felt his excitement at being near her and her own butterflies did a lovely dance inside of her. Once again there were feasts and revelry full of mirth to celebrate their queen being home. Hades laughter, echoing through the halls as the light in his eyes shone once again.

Persephone was loved by all, but especially for the magic that she wrought on Hades soul. Those that had lived in the underworld with Hades had never seen him in such a positive state of mind. He had been so driven for power and prestige that he had forgotten partly why he had chosen to fall. He wanted to experience the joys of being and feeling, of touch, taste, sound and deep thought. Unfortunately each of those things should come with a disclaimer about the positive as well as the negative.

The time came, once again for Persephone to go up above. Hades had never doubted, not one fear passed his mind, that she would chose to leave him again. The time had been full of joy and love.

They were in the great room, snuggled together in front of the fire with all three of Cerberus heads snoring softly. She held his hand, telling him how she would miss him. He felt an icy grip on his heart and as well as punch in his stomach.

He rose, without saying a word, releasing her hand from his, and went to his chamber. He was not there in the morning to see her off as he was busily drinking a morning toddy. Hades was not the sort to toy with, even though in Persephone's defense she was simply who she was, the goddess of agriculture. She could not change that or she would no longer be her.

She dearly loved Hades by now and was hurt by his response, frustrated that he could not accept her for who she was and that she too had responsibilities to those around her. Hades, on the other hand could not see the truth, but rather saw it as a deep betrayal. Where there were no walls around his heart with her before, he began to build them, high and wide. This had happened one too many times. It is unfortunate that Hades had only cared for himself for so long that he could no longer see life through the eyes of the other party, choosing to be the victim rather than finding a path that would wind together. It had to be his way, always. He picked the wrong goddess for this way of thought.

The last time that Persephone had left he stuck to drink as his coping mechanism, loving her enough that he would not take anyone else into their bed, wanting to give her all of him as he felt that this is what she deserved. Before Persephone Hades loved beautiful women as another intoxicating addiction, often having more than one a night. That first night after she left his bed was as full as his cup all night, trying to remove the pain that gnawed at his heart like Cerberus on stray cats.

Osephus told Dahlia, "The master has not shown such emotion in many centuries, I fear he will not forgive Persephone for this." Dahlia laid her head on his shoulder, happy that she could stay with him but troubled that she may be taken if things continued the way that they were headed.

Osephus assured her that as Hades love faded his realization that he still "owned" Persephone, thanks to the pomegranate seeds, would grow. His wounded pride would not allow his wife to wander permanently away, until death do they part. "We will have to be more diligent that he does not see our feelings for each other, especially in this state of mind, or he will see to it that we are separated, especially in his current state of mind."

In the weeks that followed Hades threw lavish banquets and parties, never having an empty glass or bed. Osephus marveled that Hades was able to manage the underworld so well in such a state of mind. Sure, it was not functioning at the capacity it hitherto had, but it was still functioning in a profitable manner for Hades.

Those first two months after Persephone left Hades stayed drunk and bedded as much as possible in between his duties. Problems in Osephus world did not arrive until Hades began to feel again. It was noticed first in Hades level of irritability, being a slow, upward incline of sorts. Hades was becoming accustomed to the large amounts of alcohol, making its effect not as astounding as in the beginning. Causing Hades to feel what he did not want to, grief, pain and rejection. His mind going back to his personal hell loop, Persephone left, Sara chose not to come. He did not want to think about all of these painful events, he didn't want to think, yet here he was, thinking.

If he had just been honest with himself, he knew why Persephone could not be with him year round, he just could not bring himself to see the bitter reality of it all, for that would point a finger back at him, and some of the poor choices that he had made. This would start a string of self loathing, no one loathed Hades more than he loathed himself at times. His inner dialogue would have been a shock to even Osephus.

The cycle with Persephone lasted several years. She would come home, they would love, and she would leave, each year Hades growing more bitter and building his walls higher. He was afraid to stay in that love because when she left it was so very painful. It was easier to keep a steady stream of alcohol with beautiful women flowing.

The months that Persephone was home he spent less time with her. At first this hurt her to the center of her being. Bitter was the sting when the day came that she saw another woman leave his chamber, a human no less. She had been in the underworld for several weeks, not even seeing Hades in passing.

Once again, I could go on here of how Persephone created her own legacy in the underworld, how she won, well earned, the respect of so many. But it is not her story that we are telling, but that of Hades and the morning star. So we will leave the story of Persephone, what she accomplished, created, for another book, while turning our attention back to Osephus, where Hades attention was becoming more focused on.

Hades had grown bored with his addictions. Much like cat and mouse he was tormenting Osephus, who was being very careful about keeping his relationship with Dahlia private by keeping Hades occupied while they spent time together. This was getting increasingly more difficult.

Osephus knew that there would be unspeakable consequences if Hades found out. Osephus had never been in love like this, but had become very fond of a lovely human girl centuries before. Hades was horrified on several levels, a human! He had her sent top side, which was lovely for the girl, but not for Osephus.

"You cannot focus on your real duties with such nonsense, they are trouble, I did you a favor" was thrown from Hades mouth at him.

Osephus clenched his fist at the memory and then shuddered. He loved Dahlia, he planned on spending the rest of their unnatural long lives together, whether Hades liked it or not. Hades being bound to Persephone was a joy to Osephus, not only because it ensured that Dahlia would stay with him, but also that for once, Hades scheming back fired in his face.

Hades current infatuation with Osephus was putting a damper on the song he had been humming, getting in the way of the happiness that Osephus had been enjoying. On a particularly trying day full of demands for Hades instant gratification, Sara came to Osephus mind. It was more of an accident, really, as he had not thought of her since the arrival of Persephone and Dahlia.

He loved Persephone and did not want to betray her, she had brought him the greatest gift of his life. In Dahlia he found acceptance and healing. The lust for power faded away in the shadow of love.

Every time Osephus had seen Persephone's face that first winter that Hades started with the entourage of women, he could not bear the pain that would flash across it. Only ever for a fleeting moment would anything pass across her face, as the queen of hell was not one to let her emotions outwardly show. Osephus had vowed that he would never bring that look to Dahlias face, or Persephone's. They were too good for such treatment.

It was Hades that brought up Sara's name, bringing her to mind. He had called Osephus to his great room, the fire was crackling while Cerberus heads were all snoring softly in front of it, as they were wont to do. This had made at least a dozen times that Hades, very intoxicated, had called Osephus to his great room in the last few hours. Through blood shot eyes and what Osephus was pretty sure, and certainly wouldn't say, looked like tears, Hades looked at him.

"Go to the Oracle, find Sara for me." Osephus felt a gut punch before he felt a slight amount of relief as his brain caught up with what was going on.

In a way, this was a relief as the Oracle already knew what had happened to Sara. It would guard the fact that he and the Oracle had already gone through all of this previously, while keeping the knowledge from Hades, which was in fact a very dangerous game to play. It would also help Hades to snap out of his current level of misery, which would be helpful to Osephus and his sore feet from running.

But Persephone.. he did not in any way want to betray the queen of hell. She had been so kind to keep he and Dahlias secret. His face lit up as his mind once again caught up (years of being told how to think slows your own thinking process down) and he realized if he was forced to do it then it was not betrayal. Dahlia, would of course, vouch for him in this when Persephone returned home. He asked Hades how soon he would like this done.

Once again Hades raised teary, blood shot eyes to his while he bellowed "Now!" Wherein Osephus fled the room while Hades muttered about the disregard for the importance of time.

Osephus halted on his way to the Oracles house, looking carefully around he knocked on Persephone's door. It was late, he did not want to scare her, but he was determined to have her know that this was not his doing. She opened her door, a smile lighting her face, then falling as she saw it was not Hades. It had been so long since Hades had come to her or called for her, but she still held hope.

Osephus with his inner turmoil churning had not noticed her face at all, but began to blurt everything out as he squeezed past her into her room, pausing only for the few questions that Persephone asked him here and there. She cupped his face in her hands while kissing his forehead, thanking him for his love and loyalty. He could not see the tears in her eyes as she told him that he had no choice but to do as Hades asked. Because of his one act of loyalty (Persephone knew the great risk he took to betray Hades confidence) she saw to it that he and Dahlia lived out their days together, keeping it as a tryst from Hades.

Osephus shuffled away quickly, beginning to look out of his peripheral vision to find the Oracles house. He was usually impressed as well as annoyed at how well she stayed hidden. He had been knocking for a long while before he heard one of her creatures come to the door first. He squeezed his eyes shut in anticipation of the murder that was surely to follow. Thankfully it was the Oracle who got to the door first, her pets peering around her warily. Groggily she motioned him in as it was now the middle of the night.

"And what can I do for Hades tonight?" she asked.

"He is asking for Sara", Osephus replied.

There had been a good amount of time since the Oracle had last found that Sara was now Luece. Since she had become the daughter of an ocean god her life span would be longer than a human, but that did not factor in all the other ways that one could die that were not old age.

He followed her to her room of divination, moving plants from his face that hung throughout the house. He was trying to keep an eye on the Oracles pets out of his peripheral vision, especially Callod. His seaweed colored hair seemed to wave back and forth as he stalked Osephus, who told himself he was sure it was a game, despite the glistening look in Callod's eyes.

The catlike creature was enjoying the obvious discomfort that Osephus was feeling. It was a game of cat and mouse, he knew he could not pounce on the funny little man, as that would make his mistress cross, but this was still very enjoyable. So Callod played on while the Oracle pulled her runes to divine were Sara was. If she were still Luece, or someone else entirely.

The runes divulged that she was still Luece, a water nymph and daughter of Oceanus. The guides went on to show the Oracle what ocean she was at and where to find her. She wrote it all down, handing the paper to Osephus.

She saw the inner turmoil of his soul as he took it from her. The Oracle had very few interactions with Persephone. This had been done on purpose, it was best to not get too attached to persons in the underworld. Her pets would out live her she hoped, they had already lived several centuries together with her, so she did not struggle with the information as Osephus did.

She patted his hand and spoke, "You cannot help what the master asks you to do, but you know as well as I do its best to simply do it if you would like to continue your existence, which it looks like you have enjoyed more of late." She winked at him, making the thought of Dahlia bring him back to his senses.

He shook off his feelings of betrayal, smiling at the Oracle while taking his leave. Hurrying back to Hades he found him passed out. Would Hades even remember what he had asked Osephus to do?

It was best to not risk it, the Oracle had been right, these had been the happiest years of Osephus life. He had unconditional love. He woke up with a melody dancing through his soul and fell asleep to its notes at night. His life had become one of wonder and gratitude even in the darkness of the underworld. He would hold that dear and not jeopardize it for anything.

That is where he and Hades differed the most, why he could not rise (or fall) to the heights that Hades had. He was not power hungry to the point of all else being a mute discussion, not driven to rule the world or even take your best cattle. Hades had often scorned him for this. But here was Hades, for all his pomp and show, a drunken heap passed out in his great chair with a bit of drool trickling from the corners of his mouth.

Osephus felt that he could do without that type of power. He paused, if he did not wake him and tell him what he had found out there would most likely be unpleasant consequences to follow. Osephus cleared his throat, nothing happened.

Realizing the fruitlessness of anything other than aggression, with a small amount of joy, he kicked him, swiftly jumping back while trying not to look as if his life were over. Hades sat up swiftly, which cause him to vomit. Thankfully, the vomiting made it irrelevant as to how he was awoken. He looked puzzled at Osephus for a moment before remembering. He waved for Osephus to come closer to tell him what he had found.

So Osephus revealed everything that he knew, careful to make it sound as if he had all just learned it now. He spoke of how Sara had fallen twice, once becoming the morning star, here Hades smiled, even with his eyes, replying, "she likes to help things find their way and grow, she likes to create and just be, that is fitting for her."

Osephus then told how she fell again, becoming Luece, an ocean nymph, daughter of Oceanus, titan of the sea. Hades face fell, why had she not come to see him? Osephus had been pleased by his masters happier train of thought, he would have to reign that back in, so he explained to Hades what the Oracle had shared with him, that with each time we fall, or chose to come again ,we forget a little more of where we came from and who we are.

"Sara, most likely, does not remember that she is Sara, the Oracle said that she spent several centuries as the morning star."

This was sufficient enough to put Hades back in a better mood. He would just find her, then remind her of who she truly was. Osephus scrunched his eyebrows together in thought, he was not sure that it would be that easy to accomplish, but Hades was effervescent and Osephus thought it may be good to ride the coat tails of this for a moment.

Which he did right up until the moment that Hades told him he would be the one to actively go find Luece. That meant no evenings or mornings with Dahlia for a while. He sighed, he could not refuse, that was not even an option.

Hades went on to tell him that he only trusted Osephus with this because he knew that Osephus loved Sara also. This was true, before the fall they had all been friends. One could not help but love Sara, she was light from the creator, a piece of creator that would flit around laughing, and well, creating.

Because they had been of the same breath Osephus would occasionally try to find that love in Hades, that goodness. He felt it was in the way he looked the other way when it came to Dahlia. Osephus felt the king of the underworld must know, but chose to ignore it. Osephus was grateful for this, that Hades did not put a stop to it.

Hades patted Osephus shoulder, it was more of a slap, really. Telling him to go ahead and gather supplies. Osephus hid his disappointment that he could not tell Dahlia goodbye, but did as he was told and started his journey to find Luece, the ocean nymph of Hades heart. Hades morning star.

PART EIGHT

It calls to me in the wind, the salt air caresses my cheek.

The vibration of its greatness replenishes my soul when weak.

I hear it in my dreams, the whoosh of its great breath.

I feel it in my veins, the excitement it begets.

My Ocean.

Brilliant, glorious miles of strength,

calling, singing the melody of my wait,

for the sun to rise upon its shores of sand.

No comparison to any parcel of land,

is my Ocean.

I will dance on its shores, being one with its might,

as I feel with its creation, born of new sight..

a oneness, a kinship with its ebb and flow of tide,

my ocean that calls me, home to abide.

Luece was one of the many daughters of Oceanus, at the moment her white blonde hair was pulled up on her head in a pile, her eyes full of joy as she hummed while gathering sea weed for a meal. Her mother, Tethys, had scolded her on many occasions, telling her that there were lesser nymphs, as she called them, to do the job. Luece would smile, kissing her mother, then move off to do what the "lesser" nymphs were supposed to do, while humming. She giggled to herself as she thought of this.

She did not hold to the same ideology that her parents did. She realized, rather felt, a oneness with all. She took pleasure in the simple tasks that her mother felt beneath her. There was something melodic about washing her clothes even, though cooking was her favorite as she would create something new every time. She put things together that their cook would not even think of. Her father would eat it, saying it was the best in the land, making Luece happy. She had created something that brought joy to the ones that she loved the most.

Several centuries had passed since we had last seen Luece, she still had no recognition of who she had been or where she had came from beyond the current life that she lived. Perhaps it was because she was so full of joy, feeling life was a delicious buffet of moments that she simply could not get enough of. She was happy in her present moments, relishing the now.

She had many brothers and sisters, they were often very open to the ideas that she would come up with, whether it were a new game that she had invented or a day of exploration in their ocean. If you met her, you loved her, men certainly did. She was spoken of by the humans that did business with Oceanus as his most beautiful daughter, and as mentioned, he had many.

Nymphs are known for their promiscuity, Luece was no exception. She did not have one lover, she had many, nymph and human alike. This tended to keep her schedule full, but she never wandered far from the ocean, it being her one true love. Its strength, depth, overwhelming power. It could crush you with its brute strength or carry you to safety. It was glorious and she felt it as part of her very being.

She was still gathering her seaweed, humming, when she spotted out of the corner of her eye a short man. He was very pale with dark hair and very dark eyes. She stood, brushing her thin skirt free of sand, and met his eyes. They were looking at her nervously. She smiled, asking if he needed help.

Osephus had hoped by some miracle of all the gods that she would simply recognize him, he would take her home then and it would all go smoothly from there. This was a time before we had photographs to show us how we have changed over time. Osephus had changed greatly in appearance from what he had looked like before his fall. Had she remembered who she was or where she came from she still would not have recognized her old friend, the years of tormenting service to Hades taking a toll on his physical as well as mental appearance.

Osephus introduced himself cordially, hoping that every word he spoke would jar her memory, if not, this may prove more difficult than what he had pondered on the way here. He had hoped to arrive home within the next week, back to the arms of his Dahlia. He shook himself, he had to stay on topic.

He told her of his master, Hades, she mentioned that she had heard of him. He stated that Hades would like an audience with her. As she smiled her eyes narrowed a little, she was sweet and kind, but not naïve. She had learned throughout her dealings with men, be they human or other, that caution was well to carry with her. She was all about a lovely romp but had no desire to be owned. Her freedom to be who she chose to be, that was too precious to give up.

Hades reputation preceded Osephus to her by a few decades. She remembered that he was married as well as the story of how he took his lovely wife. She had heard of his entourage of beautiful women that he enjoyed with his marriage status. She was by no means one to judge, but she liked to be in charge of such things and she did not feel that Hades was open to anyone other than himself being in charge. Still smiling she asked Osephus if he would like any refreshments after such a long journey. He sighed, he might as well since this was not going to be the short trip that he had hoped for.

Oceanus had a large house by the side of the ocean, the size of an amphitheater, to house all of his children while entertaining guests as well. The servants quarters were in a smaller dwelling off to the side. They were not to far from it, for this Osephus was grateful as he was so tired he felt it in his bones.

He watched her as she fixed food for him herself, not even looking for a servant. He looked at her intently, trying to find the Sara that he remembered. Her outward appearance gave no hint as to who she was, but her eyes, the light that had shown out of them was still a beacon for a lost soul, that had not changed. He watched as she put things together with the same vigor for creation that he had seen so many centuries ago. As the time passed he felt, he knew that she was Sara.

He asked her questions about herself, what she enjoyed, what she did with her days. Her face lit up at this, she seemed to be glowing as she answered him. He wished that he could just ask her outright if she remembered being Sara, but the Oracle had cautioned him on this, telling him that he would only look like an unreliable person, since she would not remember. When it was time for her to remember it had to be her that instigated it.

She asked about his life, this took him by surprise. No one, especially the daughter of a titan, would ask about him, given his status in this life. He told her what he liked to do, what he liked to eat. He didn't really have time for hobbies with the role that he filled. He told her a little of Dahlia. She smiled as his face showed the love he felt while he spoke. He left out some minor details of he and Dahlias meeting, such as Persephone. He even spoke of the Oracle, as he considered her his friend.

Luece listened while they munched on the meal she prepared. Osephus noticed that she truly listened to what he was saying. It was not some feigned politeness, she was taking it all in while counter questioning him.

They finished and she cleaned up, telling Osephus to rest as his journey had been long. When she turned from what she was doing she noticed the look of wonder on his face. She laughed, "You are wondering why I did not leave it for the servants? Why should I when I am quite capable myself?'

They had a lovely afternoon, she showed him her favorite spots on the shore. She swam while he rested. He was in that moment grateful that Hades had sent him. Other than Dahlia not being there it had been a lovely day. At least right up until he was ready to go home and Luece refused to go with him. He had not foreseen her saying no. He should have though, he thought to himself, after all Persephone certainly had not jumped at the chance either.

He asked her to reconsider, her eyes twinkled as she replied, "the ocean is my home, Mr. Hades may come and visit me like a gentlemen, if he would like an audience with me."

As worried as Osephus was about repercussions, he admired her nonchalant attitude. She had no fear, you could tell by her body posture that there would be no changing of her mind. He went to

shake her hand, once again she surprised him with a hug, giggling as she said, "thank you for a lovely afternoon."

This brought a blush to his cheeks and love to his heart, as he saw Sara in Luece. He pondered this all the way back to the underworld. She was Sara, he could see it. She had always been caring, feeling that everyone was one, part of the creator and part of themselves, but one with each other. She saw gods as well as poor fishermen as holy men. This was at times her downfall, but she had been loved as the angel Sara for it. Then, as the morning star, she shown her light on peasants and kings alike, leading them home safely. As Luece she did not see your station or title, your wealth, but she did see your greatness.

Each one of us has a magnificence that lays dormant inside of us. What we do with that is often shaped by our surroundings. Whether we ever see the greatness or not is greatly influenced by who we chose to keep close us and what energy we put into finding our own truths. That is the part of the person that Luece saw, and loved. That is why she was respected by all.

Her parents favored her for this as well, though their own belief's were a far cry from Luece's. They saw it as a form of charity, smiling on her giving ways while the people lived her. She was their light in the sea. Osephus rolled this thought around as well. The titan was not going to willingly hand over his favorite daughter. It seemed that Hades had a type. He wondered that Luece did not remember who she was but that she was still who she had been.

Hades was livid that Osephus came home empty handed. Persephone had not been too far away when Osephus had arrived home. Being privy to the whole plan she had been curious to meet Luece. When she heard Hades yelling she rightly assumed that Osephus had come home empty handed. She knocked on Hades door, he bellowed out, "what!"

She walked into his room, careful not to show on her face that she knew anything. Hades had enough respect left for her that he did not want to hurt her, therefore he did not want her to know what he was up to. They would figure it all out as they went along, was his motto. Since Luece was not here now, there was no point in dredging that all up now. He smiled, bowing before her, asking what he could do for his lovely wife. She took his arm, apologizing for her interruption and asking if he would like to brunch with her. Charmed by her ways, as well as lonely inside, he agreed.

Persephone looked over her shoulder, winking at Osephus who then scurried off to tell Dahlia of his adventures. He was grateful to Persephone for helping him in the moment. He shuddered, Hades beatings were getting harder to snap back from. I would assume after a millennia or so that ones resilience is just not what it used to be. This was holding true in Osephus case.

In the evening a happier Hades called Osephus to join him. He calmly asked Osephus where, exactly, did he find Luece, as well as more questions about her lack of recognition. He ended his part of the conversation by saying that perhaps Luece did not remember who she was through Osephus because he had changed so much, especially in appearance.

Osephus looked back at Hades, harder than he intended to, feeling it was almost worth the beating to comment that he was not the only one. Hades took that moment to mention that they would leave in the morning and bring Luece back home with them.

The king of the underworld, as we have seen, had to have his way, no matter the casualties. Osephus knew that Luece would not just willingly come with them, nor would she be tricked as Persephone had. Either she would remember who Hades was, (lets be real, that seemed his only hope) or she would stay exactly where she was. Osephus tried to hide his smile as he thought to himself that he would not miss this for anything.

In the morning they set off to find Luece, so confident was Hades that he brought an extra horse for the return ride home. Luece was in the ocean, playing with the sea creatures that she loved when they arrived. She recognized Osephus from his previous trip and waved. Hades assumed that she had recognized who he was already, his heart beating faster while heat crept up his face. She dried off and bounded over, hugging Osephus, he blushed, catching Hades look of fury. Hades had recognized his Sara, and his soul was on fire.

She turned to him, pushing out her hand. He was unfamiliar with a handshake. She had learned it from the humans, enjoying the cordiality that it brought. His face fell, no hug, he glared at Osephus saying, "Sara, it is me, Samiel."

She looked puzzled and then smiled, perhaps he had too much sun? "I am Luece and I thought you were Hades." She giggled.

His words, his eyes, his being, it stirred something in the depths of her, something that she had not felt in this lifetime. As if there were a voice calling, a voice that she had always known, but could no put a name to. She did enjoy how being near Hades made her feel, a bit like her ocean.

There was a safety about him that made her soul feel at home. Had she said what she felt out loud, Osephus would have laughed over the thought of Hades being associated with the word safety until he was beaten. Thankfully, she only pondered the words and what they meant in the moment.

Hades frowned at the knowledge that she truly did not remember him. How could she not remember? They were created from the same breath. She was the breath in, he the breath out. Luece, being who she was, felt his unease. For reasons that she herself did not know, she wanted to see him happy, so she took them both by the hand, leading them to her sea creatures. Today it was a dolphin, sea turtle, a few crabs and a handful of sea gulls. Hades smiled, she was still Sara, still creating.

She was busy making habitats with food reservoirs. The creatures loved and trusted her, she embraced them for what they were, loving them for it. In that moment Hades shocked Osephus by offering to help her. Her eyes lit up with her smile. She had heard some terrible things of the god of the underworld amongst gods and men, but see how kind he was! Once again, Luece being Luece, only saw the absolute best of Hades. More than what he saw in himself.

They had a lovely day together, full of laughter and creation. When it was over Hades asked, well, begged really, for her to come home with them. She took his hand, answering that it had been a lovely day, but that the ocean was her home, she fell ill if she were away from it to long. She hugged Osephus, thanking him for his time, then hugged Hades. In that moment he was no longer a power hungry god, stepping on the heads of others to achieve what he felt was greatness, he was Samiel, nestled in the arms of his Sara, his person.

In that moment the world made sense, he remembered with entirety who he was and where he had come from. He would not take away from that by trying to coerce or force Luece to come home with him. No matter how he loved her. He knew as well that she was Oceanus favorite daughter of his many, this would be no easy task. It would be best to go home and ask the Oracle for a more concrete way of moving forward. They bid their farewells, riding off with their extra horse, rider less.

Luece sat in the sand, her eyes now wide. She had felt Hades love, through that love she remembered. She remembered everything. She remembered being the morning star while somewhere, as if it were a dream within a dream, she remembered Samiel. She remembered being Sara, feeling the same arms that she just felt, seeming what was now an eternity before. She remembered their connection as soon as she felt it. A cord so strong it lasted through time.

Oceanus did not have an Oracle, but he did have a sea witch. He, as well as his many children, went to see her when they had questions that they could not answer. She used sea shells as a means of divination, asking her guides around her for guidance as well as direction. She looked very old, but no one knew her age, only that she had always been there. Eyes that were once bright blue, dimmed to grey, hair as white as the shells she used so lovingly. She was very short, though it may have seemed worse because she was so stooped over. She loved Oceanus as well as all of his children.

Luece was met with excitement when she entered her cave. They hugged, exchanging cordialities before Nianna asked what she could help Luece with. Luece shared the happenings of the day with her, asking for guidance and clarity. "How can I remember something that never happened?" Luece asked.

"It happened, just not in this lifetime," Nianna replied. She went on to explain the fall to Luece, how each lifetime we forget a little more of who we are and where we came from.

"Some of us remember, we remember every lifetime, but more forget, always feeling that there is something in the back of their mind, something that they have misplaced. Hades, or Samiel, whichever you would like to call him, helped you remember because of the deep connection that you share. Moving those latent memories to the front of your mind," Nianna said.

Nianna, using her shells, was able to gather most of the story for Luece. This was a lot for the ocean nymph to process, making the next few days difficult. In her frustration she went to her mother, asking what she new of these matters. Tethys smiled, agreeing with Nianna, telling Luece that she was in her first life after the fall, as many of the gods and titans were, their lifespan being so much longer with the intention that they had set. Luece felt that this was a good time to bring up Hades and his connection to her.

Tethys scowled as Luece prattled on, not looking at her mothers face. Tethys had let Luece be Luece since she was small, sometimes having to defend her actions to Oceanus. Especially in the way that Luece showed equality to all. Tethys saw it as charming and different, Oceanus feared that it was weakness on his favorite daughters part. Tethys would argue that it was good for the world to see such kindness from the titans daughter, especially since Oceanus was not overly disposed to kindness himself. He may even have invented the caste system.

"Everyone has their place," he would bellow, "most of them are beneath me."

This would bring laughter to gatherings, and though it upset Luece, she loved and accepted her father for who, and what , he was. A titan. Truth be told the titan was very proud of his different daughter, the light that she shown to any and all. When she laughed the world smile, himself included. For that she would always have a special place in his heart, even through the following days and years that followed.

Tethys knew that Oceanus would not be okay with the mighty Hades knocking on the door of his realm, especially in regards to his favorite daughter. No matter what lives they lived before. Luece being so fascinated by Hades planted fear in her mother heart. She reminded Luece gently, of how sea nymphs could never be far from the ocean. It was the mighty ocean that fed, powered, their longevity. It was the ocean that kept their vibration high, eradication sickness and disease from their bodies. Luece had never had a day of sickness in her abnormally long life.

In the days that followed Luece could not get Hades out of her mind. She visited Nianna often to finish piecing together who she was. This helped her remember details more vividly. She remembered Samiel, the love that they shared, their dreams, goals and days of creating together. It dawned on her that her promiscuity was not only because she was a sea nymph, but because she had been looking, searching, for that feeling of kinship and oneness that she has felt with Samiel.

She sat on the edge of her ocean as the sun rose in the morning, crowning the edge of the sky with the glories of creation in reds and pinks. She sat remembering, feeling all that she remembered. It troubled her that Samiel had become Hades.

Her father loved power, in many ways she had seen him act far worse than the stories that she had heard of Hades. She remembered Samiel being envious of those with power on their trips of creation, the memories still with a fog around them. He would talk about how unfulfilling creating was without great power. She would smile at him, sometimes with a laugh, and ask, "if you were meant to create, why do you need more power? How does that enhance creation? It seems that it would only enhance you."

That had been their last "almost" argument, before Samiel fell, becoming Hades. The ocean washed over her legs as she remembered being the morning star, the many people that she had led home in the darkness when they had lost their way. They only had to look up to see her light. Honestly, that part had been the most frustrating because many of them never thought to look up, so invested in their fear they could not look beyond their feet. Had they paused to simply look up, they would have found their way.

Her missing of Samiel was what put an end to her time as the morning star, the defining factor in her decision to fall again. She asked Nianna if humans had originated like that as well. "We all

133

have, all born of the beauty and love of creator. All once angels that created with the creator. But one by one this was not enough for the chaos that stirred in the heart of us. Without chaos though, there would be no creation. We chose to fall then, some being better at manipulating their fall, becoming gods, titans and giants, living centuries. Others simply wanted something different, to experience senses, they became humans, living the life span of a wink in time compared to gods and titans. They were easily swayed by their fear, which was used to manipulate and control them then. They added power to those that craved power by reacting to their fears."

Luece thanked her, hugging her and leaving a kiss on her withered cheek. She wandered in thought for a time, finding herself on the edge of the ocean where Hades found her, and she ached for him. Bending over, she wrote in the sand: "My soul cries out to your soul through the depths of time, from portals not seen, I feel you even when you are not here." She secretly hoped in her chest that he would feel her call, much as he used to feel her before the fall, as she etched it all in the sand.

Meanwhile, Hades had gone to see the Oracle with Osephus in tow, asking her many of the questions that Luece had asked Nianna while adding a few of his own. "How could she not recognize me? How could she not remember me?"

The Oracle gave him many of the same answers that Nianna had given to Luece. This felt like insufficient information in the light that it did not bring Luece home to him. So it was, that while he was in his chair, in his great room pondering all that he learned while Cerberus many heads snored, he felt the call of Luece.

She had never uttered anything out loud, but her soul had cried for its other half, that half heard. Tears ran down Hades face as he felt it, the memories flooding his soul, as he remembered who he was and where he came from. You will most likely not read this little tidbit of information any where else, but for the first time in a millennia, he felt shame and guilt for what he had become. His beautiful Sara, his light, his own morning star that seemed to beacon him home, had turned the light back on.

PART NINE

There are moments when darkness descends on our souls and minds.

There are moments of fear and worry, some things that we no longer find.

Such as peace and beauty, direction for our words to say.

We have forgotten how to ask, we have forgotten how to pray.

Reach for the stars, the pin pricks of light

that shine in your darkness, that glow through your night.

And when it is so dark that you cannot see your feet,

look up to the sky where the stars will greet,

where once again you will find your way

no matter the depths of the darkness,

the stars will guide you to day,

if you allow light to be your stay.

Hades barely had the sense to wait until morning, perhaps the remembering brought with it the clarity to think of others a little more once again, or perhaps he had simply been too tired to travel. He woke Osephus up by shaking him, this brought a yelp from Osephus as it was not their usual morning routine. Osephus was grateful that it was not a night that Dahlia had stayed with him, she having things to do for Persephone that took her away earlier than normal. Hades had covered his mouth mid yelp, he did not want to wake Persephone up as he was still struggling with the strange emotion of guilt. He was hoping by ignoring said emotion he could once again be rid of it.

He did an astounding job with hand motions to convey to Osephus what he wanted. It was enough that Osephus knew to get up and get dressed, which was the first step anyway. The sun was just coming up as they left the underworld, once again with an extra horse in tow. Hades had felt Luece all night, he was sure that this time she would come home with him. The thought of Persephone was still a tap in the back of his thoughts, but he felt like things would unfold as they went along. Why stir anything up before things were concrete to begin with?

Luece was sitting on the shores of her ocean while the sun burst up over the horizon. She was humming a song that she had written, inspired by the love she had for her ocean. The words are as follows:

I can hear it as it calls me, it beckons me from shore.

I can feel its pull from its mighty waves, it draws from me, more.

It burns in my blood, the rush of the ocean tide.

I can hear it in my heart beat, where it flows, it resides. I watch it in the sunset, I see it in the stars, it moves my very being, it draws me from afar.

My ocean.

Oh sky so blue with waters that are deep, I feel your beckoning call, In the beauty of my dreams, in every step that falls..

My ocean.

In addition to her normal morning joy she felt something else, something that she was not familiar with. It was longing. She had never longed for anything as all that she loved was at her fingertips. At this moment though, what she longed for was not there. Her ocean had a rival. She pushed it aside while singing her song out loud, once more, before seeking out Nianna to ask her of the strange emotions that stirred inside of her.

Nianna listened intently, interjecting explanations here and there. The sea witch had seen what was coming for Luece. She was curious to see how it would affect the paths of everyone involved, but she knew not to interfere. Everyone had their own path, their own journey, that they walked. Often we are searching for the destination, not realizing that the destination is the journey itself, or we never would have chosen to come in the first place.

Luece thanked her for her time and headed back to the shore, feeling the intensity of her longing growing. Without knowing what she was doing she turned in the direction of Hades, closing her eyes, feeling for him. He was still a days journey away, but he felt it. The tug at his heart. The adaptability of his mind to push everything from it but her.

As the sun rose in the sky, so did their excitement. Hades knew where his stemmed from, he was headed that way. Luece only felt that something big, fantastic, was about to happen. She could not place her finger on it. She could feel it in her being as she went to bed, then throughout the morning, as she went about her rituals.

She was out, once again tending to her sea creature friends when she felt him. She turned, he was still a blur in the distance he was so far away, but she knew who it was. Her feet ran over the sand, as fast as she could go to meet him. He jumped from his horse and they stood for a moment, just looking at each other, with pure joy on their faces. They were once again Samiel and Sara in that moment, two parts of one whole. There was nothing else.

They had never physically touched before, energetically they had always been connected, making it easy to feel each other even when they were far away. Luece threw herself in his arms and he held her near, afraid that she would evaporate like a mirage. Tears ran down his face, hitting her head. She did not care what anyone thought or said of him, he was her Samiel, the other half to her breath of life. He was her beginning and may possibly be her ending, but his tears were proof that he still felt.

They stepped apart, interlacing and releasing their fingers, feeling ecstasy in that simple gesture of physical touch that they had never experienced with each other. Osephus watched with wonder on his face. He had never seen Hades so vulnerable since before the fall. Nor had he seen such a look of joy on the king of darkness face. Luece moved her hands to his face, taking in his dark eyes, feeling the softness of his dark beard. He cupped her face in his hands in return, kissing her. It was the kiss of surrender. She was his morning star, guiding him from the depression that he had been feeling since what he felt to be Persephone's betrayal.

It was getting dark out, Luece knew that her parents would worry if she did not go home soon. She laced her fingers through Hades, resting her head on his shoulder as they walked back to the Titans large home. Osephus fidgeted nervously, wondering how this was going to play out. His thoughts wandering form Oceanus to Persephone. Why did Hades somehow complicate everything?

Tethys had told Oceanus what Luece had shared with her about Hades and their origin together. Oceanus had never been fond of Hades, his reputation and lust for power preceding him everywhere. Most of Oceanus daughters were not married. This was partially because nymphs are promiscuous, getting bored with one partner easily. Mainly, it was due to the fact that Oceanus had no desire to pass his crown on, especially to someone not of his own blood.

He had no intentions of his daughter, especially his favorite daughter, marrying Hades. He was convinced that somehow Hades had put this idea into his lovely daughters head. Oceanus remembered Hades fall, as well as his rise to power, then gaining the kingdom he now had, though it all happened several millennia ago. He had learned from others that the more you fall the harder it is to remember who you are and where you came from. He had seen it happen to some that had first fallen with him, loosing them twice as they did not remember who he was when he sought them out after they returned. Many of them were now human, not remembering their own divinity, only knowing him as Oceanus the mighty Titan, not friend, and definitely not equal.

With these memories he knew that it was entirely possible that the whole story was true. That did not change his mind in regards to Hades. Hades stood for everything that Luece did not. Hades dealt in death and power while Luece was flitting here and there, creating, healing, spreading love and joy, not fear or the plague of fear. That is why though Oceanus knew it could all be possible, he still did not believe it.

Oceanus was quiet when Luece brought Hades into his great room. In fact, the whole room became quiet. Osephus followed them in, being grateful for his diminutive stature. It was easier for him to hide behind Hades. Tethys took note of Luece's shining face, the love that shone from her eyes, while noting Hades calm. She wondered when Hades pushed the strong drink away, as well. She did not know that the king of the underworld wanted to feel, to remember, every encounter he had with Luece.

Hades knew that Oceanus would not simply agree to Luece going home with him. Hades loved Luece too much for trickery. Whatever was going to follow would involve her autonomy in the decision, and he, Hades, would support whatever that decision was. He had missed her too long for it to be any other way.

Some part of Luece touched Hades throughout the whole of dinner. This was new and exciting, being able to physically touch each other. She had found her Samiel, she was planning on keeping closer tabs on him this time.

After dinner Oceanus asked Hades to walk with him a moment along the shores. As the waves crashed around his voice, Oceanus told Hades that it was time for him to leave. Adding for clarity that if he truly loved Luece, Hades would leave her where she was. " You must know, that as an ocean nymph she cannot be far from the ocean or she will become mortal, and she will die as a mortal with a mortal life span."

Hades felt a pang inside of himself, an internal battle raging. He had heard tales that ocean nymphs could not be far from the ocean, but one hears many tales that do not necessarily have a true basis to them. He loved Luece, sincerely. As Samiel, he would not have put her in such danger, but he was no longer only Samiel, he was also Hades. And Hades was not a giver, he was a taker. He would lose all that he had worked for if he abandoned the underworld. He could not just pack up and live by the ocean.

Oceanus was looking out over the waves while Hades studied his face. Tall and proud, he had horns like a bull and the tail of a ser-

pentine fish where others had legs. Hades often marveled that
Oceanus got around so well.

As he studied him he thought that Oceanus could very well be
lying. Luece had always been the titans favorite, Osephus had told
Hades. That would cause him to say anything. Besides, love was
stronger than anything, he and Luece had a deeper connection than
many. With these thoughts, Hades stilled his unease that perhaps he
was hurting Luece more than helping.

Oceanus could have easily crushed Hades, he knew and respected this. So Hades continually turned the conversation to matter
he knew Oceanus could not resist input on, taking the titans mind off
of the immediate situation. Hades felt, after all, it would be Lueces final decision to make.

Tethys was singing with Luece when they returned. Their
voices rang in harmony throughout the halls. Both men stopped, a
smile crossing their faces. Hades smile faded quickly as he noted
Tethys gaze resting on Lueces face.

They looked nothing alike. Tethys hair was dark, Lueces almost
white and pulled up in dreadlocks. Tethys eyes were an aquatic green
while Lueces were a grey blue. Luece also did not sport the pair of
wings on her forehead that her mother did. Hades was never sure why
they were there. To be sure he wondered often at the choices the titans had made during their own creation process. Much of it did not
seem attractive to him.

Luece smiled when her eyes caught his, she jumped up, running to him. This brought a scowl to her fathers face. Luece did not
read the room as she had eyes only for Hades. She had missed him for
so long, not even realizing that she missed him. She was not going to
lose him now.

Tethys had told her daughter when she was younger that if she left the ocean mortality would settle on her. That had never been a fear before, because the ocean was her first love, until she remembered the original. Until she remembered what home truly felt like. She had watched her parents faces throughout the evening, watched the displeasure, and actual disgust from her father.

She knew that they would never agree to her leaving with Hades. She rubbed her hands together in thought. Who wants to live an eternity if part of that eternity is missing, the part that made it seem alive? Her rationale was that if she became a human, dying early, she would simply find him again. It had still not settled into her mind how that each time we reincarnate, we lose a little more of the memory of who we were, becoming more difficult to find who we truly are.

Nymphs are well known for their cunning, Luece was no exception for this, and she was blessed well with the cunning. Throughout the evening she squeezed Hades hand. It was a series of squeezes manipulated by hand strength and duration of hold. After the third time Hades remembered the system, as they had used it before the fall, but in a slightly different way.

There had been a period of time in the beginning of creation, when angels were in the throes of battling for power, that Samiel and Sara had developed a system of energy movements if one felt it was time for them to leave the situation. Because two are often better than one, this had kept them safe on many occasions. Hades felt himself smiling. She was telling him it was time to go, to be safe.

Hades rose, thanking Oceanus and Tethys for a lovely evening while commenting on how early he had to rise to make it back to his duties in the underworld. Luece feigned disappointment as they all stood and bid him good night. Luece continued to play the part, staying with her parents.

She was genuine in the love that she showered them with that night. She knew that if she did this thing she would never see her parents again in this life, and she felt a pang of grief. To never see her ocean again.. she pushed this thought away as it was too much to feel at once.

She knew Hades was very busy, and honestly it did not even cross her mind to ask him to stay with her, even though he would have kept his immortality, making it the better choice for both. Luece was a giver, Hades got the takers half. With the passing of time it became easier to see who was what of their two halves of the whole. Who was the light, and who tended to be the dark.

If her parents ever knew that night, they did not let on, even through their emotions. Perhaps they realized the futility of it. Luece would have her way, one way or another. If she had ever been one to crave power as Hades did, she would have surpassed him in the way that once she set her mind to something, she would create that reality out of nothing, if she had to.

As the great house settled in for the night Luece gathered those things nearest and dearest that she could carry. It was a bit more than a knapsack, she was a girlie nymph. She crept down to Hades room, tapping on the door lightly. He opened it, slowly, still unsure if he had understood her correctly.

She threw her arms around his neck, kissing him. He laughed out loud, before catching himself, fearful to wake anyone up. Peeling her off of him he smiled, motioning for her to be quiet. She smiled back, nodding her head in agreement.

Osephus had been told to wait outside with the horses and to be ready to leave at any moment. He was faithfully sleeping with them. Hades stopped himself before delivering a swift kick, he did not want Luece to see that side of him. So he shook him with some extra vigor. That's a polite way to write it.

Osephus jumped up and Luece hugged him. Hades frowned, thinking he had some teaching for Luece on servants. He was more worried about leaving without waking the household at that moment.

Luece took one, last look at her ocean. She did not know it would be the last time that she saw her ocean in that life. Sorrow lingered for a moment as she watched the waves. Hades took her to other oceans during her lifetime with him, but it was too risky with the possibility of the Titans retribution to take her back to hers.

She turned, looking at Hades. Her heart was full, so full it was overflowing onto her cheeks. She was ready to move forward with him.

PART TEN

How we wander, how we labor, for the thing just around the bend.

We punch our clocks, we pay our dues, until another days end.

Caught up in the whirlwind of daily life and care,

we move away from the present, even though we are there!

Hades took Luece home to his underworld. Throughout their travel he had been pondering how their arrival may go. He, of course, had no idea of the conversation that Persephone had with Osephus. He did feel, that perhaps this was one of those moments in life that he should have put a little more thought into how events should be handled.

Luece was singing on her horse. Hades smiled to himself as he remembered her as Sara, singing to the creatures that she had helped to name. She would sing to the flowers in the morning the same tune that he heard her hum now. He would not live without her song in his life again, he vowed.

He motioned for Osephus to fall back to him. Luece was quite caught up in her present song, so Hades felt it safe to talk. He asked Osephus to ride ahead and explain the situation to Persephone. Osephus looked blankly at him, trying to decipher if this were a trap or if Hades was in earnest. "How, exactly, would you like me to explain the situation?" he asked of Hades.

"Oh, I don't know, tell her that she is some, long lost cousin. You are intelligent, you will figure it out."

Honestly, this played so well in Osephus favor that he was delighted. He loved Luece and Persephone. He did not want to betray either one of them. But this way he could continue his conversation with Persephone without having to sneak around.

He was curious as to what Luece would think of Hades being married. He did not know that Hades had already told Luece the whole truth. Hades had never kept anything from her before, he would not start now. Well, he did keep a few things to himself. He shifted in his seat with that thought.

It did not phase Luece in the least. Ocean nymphs were well know for their promiscuity. They never had only one mate, as they did not want to be owned by anyone. They were as wild, as free, as the sea that they so loved.

Luece asked Hades many questions of Persephone, especially intrigued by the story of the pomegranate seeds. She giggled at him, thinking that he could "catch" a goddess, and he smiled, sheepishly, at her humor. He was relieved that she saw humor, and not anything else.

Luece bounced on her horse, causing the poor beast some discomfort. She immediately apologized to the creature, exclaiming to Hades, " She is the goddess of agriculture, she loves to create as I do, this will be wonderful!"

Hades grew quiet over this, not having put much thought into the women being in the realm together, let alone friends. This made him uncomfortable in ways that he could not identify in that moment. He felt the best course of action was to change the subject to festivals.

Soon they were outside of the gates of the underworld. Just oust side of those gates lay a beautiful valley. Luece caught her breath, in her moment of wonder, touching Hades arm. "When I die, bury me here in this beauty."

He frowned, trying to put out of his head what Oceanus had said about her mortality if she left her ocean. In making her choice Luece knew the totality of what she was sacrificing. That's not to say that she did not grieve for her ocean the rest of that life, but she had made her decision whole heartedly, accepting all of the consequences that it brought with it. Something that Hades had not learned yet.

He was sure in his heart, that they would find some soothsayer, shaman, or spell caster that could bring Luece's immortality back to her. Then they would live together had they did in the beginning of time. So he ignored her comment of burial, holding her hand as they passed through the gates.

Osephus was sitting with Persephone. He had just finished filling her in on what had happened. He was currently answering her barrage of questions of Luece. They were coming out of her mouth as fast as he answered them.

Among the gods and goddesses nymphs were considered less than equals, much like the demi gods and goddesses, even though their parents were titans. Much of this was due to the humans beliefs, creating the fallacy that surrounded such stories. The gods had what they were due to centuries of human belief. Had the humans taken that away, had they given the divinity back to themselves, the gods would have had nothing.

Persephone had felt pangs of jealousy as Osephus mentioned Hades and Luece's connection. She realized there had to be a deep connection for Hades, and his pride, to be seen with a nymph. A nymph!! Barely above a human!

Persephone thanked Osephus for his loyalty in telling her first. Osephus kept to himself the information that Hades had asked him to tell her, he wanted to stay in her good graces for he and Dahlias sake. He bowed, rushing to find Dahlia, grateful with the realization that they would have much time together as Hades sorted his life mess for a moment.

Persephone sat in thought. It was almost time for her to go home for the seasonal change. She knew that she would outlive Luece, from what Osephus had told her. She decided that she would simply avoid Luece, the underworld was vast, it should not be a difficulty for the short amount of time yearly that she was in the underworld.

What made Persephone such an incredible leader was her ability to differentiate when it was time to advance, time to retreat, or time for a truce. She would gain nothing by belittling or abusing Luece. From what Osephus said, the girl was charming, she would definitely out live her, being then stuck with a grumpy Hades. She decided to simply make peace with Luece.

She called for Dahlia, asking her to get a dinner around that evening in honor of Luece. "Have Osephus help you," she said, winking.

Hades had brought Luece to his chambers, while hers were being prepared. She was loving on Cerberus, much to Hades amusement. Cerberus tolerated his master, loved his master, but did not let anyone else touch him. With three mouths that can bite, tear, and wreak havoc, generally no one else tried to touch him. Luece had seen him lying by the fire and skipped over to love on the large puppy as she called him.

She stopped mid petting when she felt Hades eyes on her. She turned to look at him, realizing that for the first time they were truly alone. Hades had realized it a few minutes before. He had often wondered, with their deep connection, what physically touching her would be like.

He walked the length of the room to her, she stood there, her eyes never leaving his face, but full of love and wonder. When he kissed her, he felt his entire being ignite. As her hands cupped his face, he lost his constant thought of power, his incessant need of being in control. He was simply, entirely, in that moment. Lost in the touch of unconditional love.

Dahlia knocked on Hades chamber door, he recognized the knock as hers were light and swift. As if she were already running away in case she had offended him. Upon asking her to come in there was a parchment slid under the door and fleeting steps.

Luece looked at Hades, giggling she asked, "What have you done that makes them so swift?"

He smiled at her, tucking her in closer to his arm. He did not want her to disappear again. He was honestly unsure of how Persephone was going to react to Luece. He realized how offensive of a gesture it was in bringing Luece there, but especially his bed. He had not had physical contact with Persephone in years.

He frowned as he recalled their last conversation. He had been slightly inebriated, she had just arrived back to the underworld for the season. In his pain of what he only saw as rejection when she would leave and go back to her parents, he would lash out at her. They had taken to avoiding the problem by avoiding each other. The underworld was quite large, so this was never hard to do.

Hades thought it best, due to current circumstances, to go ahead and see what was on that parchment paper. He kissed Luece's head, moving her over gently by tickling her when she tried to cuddle back into him. He felt that odd sensation again, that feeling of joy, wash over him.

He was pleasantly surprised when he read that Persephone was inviting Luece to dinner. His name was not on it, any where. He glanced at Luece, who was trying to coax Cerberus into the bed. He realized how little he truly knew Persephone, even after all the years that they had been married.

He felt very protective of Luece, as he tried to sort what Persephone may be trying to do. On one hand, she may truly be holding out the proverbial olive branch of peace. On the other hand she may be about to tear Luece up, as that would be what he would do in this situation.

He called for Osephus, who was realizing that the drama was cutting into his personal life instead of adding to it. Hades showed him the invitation, asking him what he made of it. Osephus stared at him. He could not remember a time that Hades had asked his opinion on anything, even Cerberus's collar. Osephus felt this had to be

Luece's influence, that having what others may call his "better half" had softened him.

It dawned on him that staring was not the correct answer so he replied that he thought it would be a good idea. It helped that he knew the back ground to the story. Osephus shared with Hades how Persephone had listened to the story of Luece with genuine interest.

Hades was still skeptical, but he trusted Osephus, knowing that he loved Luece almost as much as Hades did. Hades took the invitation to Luece who squealed in delight at the prospect of a dinner so soon. This brought a smile to the kings face, while he inwardly congratulated Persephone for her wisdom. Persephone had also sent Dahlia to help Luece find something to wear and get prepared, knowing that Luece would not have her own servant.

That is how Persephone met and came to know Luece, who was also Sara, who was also the morning star. They became close friends, remaining that way throughout Luece's life in the underworld with Hades. Luece missed Persephone when it was time for her to go back to Olympus, and always met her rejoicing when she came home.

Hades marveled that the women got along, but particularly with the graciousness that Persephone shown to Luece. Persephone had been very wise in this one decision, it won her something that few others had, the respect of Hades. He left many decisions in the underworld to his queen after that, and it was known among its occupants that Persephone was the one you asked the favors of, not Hades.

While Luece lived, though, Hades had eyes only for her. He had her a salt water pool made, in wild hopes that it would slow down the aging process, as well as ease the moments that she became almost ill for missing her ocean. It helped in easing her grief, but for the rest of that life she missed the sound of the waves, the cry of the seagull as the salt breeze kissed her face.

She mourned when her first wrinkles came on her face. Hades kissed them, dancing her around the room until she laughed them away from thought. His heart was heavy, though, as the shadow of reality began to cross his vision. The accountability of what he had actually done settled into his heart.

For Osephus, these were the golden years. Hades was malleable, almost kind, with Luece by his side. No more massive mood swings when Persephone left. Luece would drag them to the four corners of the underworld, meeting everyone and exploring what had never been seen while creating a new way of being for an old god.

She loved to visit the Oracle the most of all the things that she experienced in the underworld. She sat at her table upon the first meeting, Onie was right up against her with the other two pets nearby. "Onie does not usually like anyone but me, it looks as if you have changed his mind," the Oracle said.

At Luece's request the Oracle taught her the ways of divination. Luece especially loved using the runes, little rocks with symbols on each. The symbols, each meaning a multitude of truths, that spoke to you in the right moment. The Oracle told her that the spirit guides use them to direct their answers.

Luece remembered as Sara when the humans would ask her for help. She had always liked that, answering and helping them. Angels must abide by the law of freewill, so there were many times she watched on helplessly, not being able to help because she had not been asked. It helped her understand now that she was doing the asking.

Luece hugged the Oracle, thanking her for her wisdom as well as her hospitality. She kissed each pet on its forehead. This was a pleasant surprise for the Oracle, she asked Luece to come back. Luece did, frequently, becoming an apprentice, as well as a daughter for the Oracle, spending many happy hours learning with her.

Time, however, keeps marching on. With out the ocean to take away her aging Luece began to show signs of her mortality. She noticed it first, a grey hair here, a wrinkle there. She was sitting in the Oracles herb room with Callod in her lap, his seaweed hairs flickering with satisfaction at her touch, when she asked the Oracle," Will I remember again?"

The Oracle was making tea, they had been having a lovely day of learning how to read the stars while Hades was attending to matters of business. Luece had found another stiff, grey hair that morning that had her mind rolling on her mortality. She wondered if she would come back, or perhaps be an angel again. Her gnawing fear being she would not find Hades again.

"I do not know the answers to those questions, if or when you will remember. I feel you will find Hades again, you are good for each other, balancing the other out, in this life anyway. Each life is different, that makes knowing yourself the most important relationship of any life, "the Oracle said.

That was sufficient for Luece, she did not worry about things that she could not control as she had a deep love for creator, feeling that creator would fill the gaps she could not. Hades, however, did not view life the same. He felt you had to take and conquer, forget asking creator, figure it out yourself, preferably before anyone else did.

He took Luece to many different oceans, hoping that it would slow down the aging process or stop it. He dare not take her back to her own, he had heard the rumblings of how Oceanus felt about him. His life would reset the day he met the titan again, he was not eager to experience that. Even though Luece had come willingly with him, he had taken something that did not belong to him.

So though it grieved him to watch her age, he could not bring himself to face his own fears and take her back to the one place that may extend her life. Luece did not blame him for this, that never crossed her mind. She had learned a beautiful art, the art of living in the moment. In fact, the moments that Hades would voice his fears, she cupped his face in her hands and said, "Let's go to the Valley of the Gods and see what mischief we can get into!"

Hades would laugh, more than ready to shake the dread from his mind, and they would make a day of it. He also wondered what would happen when she died. Would they find each other again? The Valley days would eradicate these fears, creating what Osephus called the golden age of the underworld.

Luece lived for eighty glorious years with Hades. She truly lived every moment of those years as she never knew how long her years would be. To the gods this is the blink of an eye, so to say that Hades was not ready does not touch on the strength of emotions that he felt. It is said that he sat for a day by her bed after she passed, refusing any one else to come in, to say his good bye.

Persephone had also grown to love her, mourning deeply at that time, as well as the rest of the underworld. She had shone in that darkness, lighting Hades himself. The kingdom missed her for many years after.

Hades remembered what Luece had said the first day that she came to the underworld, of the beauty of the field that lay before. He had her buried in the Elysian fields, before the gates of the underworld. A white poplar grew above, magnificently reaching for the skies that she once hung in. Once again, Samiel longed for his Sara, wondering when they would be together again.

PART ELEVEN

In the shadows of my memories, in the corners of my mind,

I believe that we have met though I cannot seem to place the time.

Are we strangers, are we friends, lovers from long ago?

In the recess of my memory, I may never know.

You feel like a song that once I played,

the notes strong as my body swayed.

You seem like a thought I can't unthink

as we tremble on the brink

of all we know and see..

it feels as if you are part of me.

Danica was lacing up her tennis shoes. Her waitress shift started in fifteen minutes and she was in a rush after a rough night. It was her own fault, she knew. She had gone out with her friends, Lisa and Holly, drinking and at twenty three she was the least to succeed at being an alcoholic, not able to hold her liquor, as they told her. Even at the "Danica pace" as they called it.

She had been up most of the night, she was currently holding her belly in horror while getting ready. A pleasant thought took her mind off of the torture feeling in her veins from the alcohol pumping through: she only worked four hours today, she could do anything for four hours. She kissed the picture of her grandparents good bye as she ran out of the door.

She lived in the town of Beaufort North Carolina, she had her whole life. Her parents had died when she was eleven, her grandparents raising her after that. They had recently passed, her grandmother going first eighteen months ago, and her grandfather following a year after. They had been married for fifty six years making it difficult for her grandfather to know how to exist without her grandmother.

She hoped to find a love like that. Someone that you could grow old and build empires with. Her grandparents had owned a small store that they sold seafood out of for all of Danica's life. Being a coastal town Beaufort was known for its fresh seafood and Danica loved to eat it. Her grandfather would tease her that she should not eat any of it, as she could also be considered sea life with as much time that she spent in the ocean. "Cannibalism," he would say, with a twinkle in his eye, shaking his head.

She missed her family, all of her family. She had been an only child with her parents focused on their careers. Even though she loved them, she did not miss them as much as her grandparents, as her grandparents had always been her primary care takers even before her parents death in a car accident. Making their passing a dark night of her soul to pass through.

Her coping skills were non existent, causing drinking to be an easy escape from reality. The drinking had caused her to miss enough work, though, that her employer had kindly given her the name of a therapist. She had done it with so much compassion that after Danica's initial self righteous reaction, she realized that this was a step that she needed to take.

She had inherited the house with enough money to live on as well as finish college with. She just wasn't sure yet as to what she wanted to be when she grew up. Her grandparents had thought she would do something with the ocean, the way that she loved it, like a marine biologist. Her granny would leave brochures on her night stand and in her bathroom as little encouragements her and there.

Even though Danica loved the ocean and all of its creatures, that was not something that appealed to her. The brochures she left laying around though, as a reminder of her grannies love. She knew, though, that she had to come up with something as being a waitress would not pay for everything when her inheritance ran out.

Her shift was swift, for which she was grateful for. Afterwards Holly and Lisa were ready to go out and repeat the previous nights events. Danica agreed to go, because, well, what else was she going to do? That was generally how her cycle went, sleep, work, drink, get sick, then repeat.

She woke up, grabbing her head with her hands immediately. The sun was higher in the sky than it should be. She grabbed her phone, she had slept through her alarm, and her first therapy appointment was in less than fifteen minutes. She flew out of bed, where she promptly threw up from the movement. Her self dialogue was berating, full of shame and condemnation.

She splashed some water in her face at the bathroom sink. Looking in the mirror her pale blue eyes and honey brown hair were a mess. She threw some water on her hair as well, she would be only a few minutes late.

In the therapists waiting room she locked around. She was surrounded by what her granny used to call "new age" stuff. Some of it looked like it was from different countries, like Africa. It looked tribal in nature. There was a painting of the earth titled "Gaia" as well as a painting of a tree with the strangest branches labeled "The Tree of Life".

Her grandparents had been very religious, but not spiritual. Her granny had warned her of such belief systems and wandering off the path of religion that way. She had told her that way led you away from the Lord, straight to hell. This kept Danica motivated by fear to not go delving into these avenues of thought. Though she thought as she sat there, since she had never met her grannies Lord it would be difficult to wander away from him.

The door to the office opened and a tall woman appeared. She had to be over six feet, Danica thought. Danica was five foot four and had to jerk her head back to make eye contact with the woman. She had the strangest feeling as she looked into her golden brown eyes, that she knew this woman from somewhere. Her dark skin making Danica look even more pale than her drinking had done.

Her office had more new age things in it. Strange books lined the shelf with tapestries on the walls that made you feel good looking at them, but Danica had seen them no where else. She had pictures of what Danica assumed to be her cats all around her office as well. The name plate on the desk read: Maria Jeffreys.

Maria smiled as they sat down. Danica was unsure of how all of this talk therapy worked, when did she start talking? So she took the lead, blurting out most of her life story as fast as she could. She was having a difficult time since the room was blurred and spinning with many of her movements.

When she finished her story, between the stress of divulging all of her life combined with her wicked hangover, she threw up. She made it to the bowl with round, white candles in it. Her shame was written all over her red, tear stained face. "I may also have a drinking problem," she added.

Maria patted her hand, telling her she thought that she could help Danica get her life back, even get enough control to move forward in a positive way. Danica felt relief wash over her being. She had not been convinced that therapy would help her when her employer had insisted on it. She knew that it could not bring back the dead, and she felt that was what she needed more than anything.

She knew that her family had not died on purpose, but it felt as if she had been abandoned. Left to take on the whole world alone. She had not been ready to admit that small fact to anyone, even herself. Maria assured her that it was a positive step in healing.

The hour went by fast with Maria giving Danica healthy alternatives to her current choice of forget-me-nots. When Danica left she felt something that she had not felt since before her grandparents death, she felt hope. She had been missing that very important emotion.

Maria had asked Danica if she had any spiritual practices. Danica had been raised going to church, her granny being very religious. Her granny would not have approved of seeing a therapist, telling her that Jesus was enough to carry it. Going to church had only instilled fear into Danica. Fear of judgement and wrath, mixed with a little hell fire. When she shared that with Maria she was given the reply, " A connection to your creator, a daily connection will do the opposite, it will instill safety and peace through faith, hope, and love. Sometimes we forget that the connection is the most important part of spirituality We will work on finding your magnificence that you hold inside of you, Danica.

Danica liked that thought. She pondered it for several days afterwards before sharing it with Lisa and Holly. They listened as they tried to coax Danica out drinking again. "Come on Danny," Holly coaxed, "we are only young once!"

So once again, Danica went with them. Once again she was late to work from a hangover. This time her employer fired her.

Danica sat down on the curb outside of the restaurant. She was grateful that everything she owned was paid for. Her grandparents had seen to that as well as a nice sized nest egg. That was for college, though, and she would have to have a job. That had been instilled in her growing up, at an early age, from her workaholic parents.

She went to the beach to think. She found the sound of the waves hitting the shore cleared her mind. She felt the peace and joy wash over her as the salt water breeze blew out her hair. The sea gulls song played in harmony with the crash of the waves, and slowly her panic left her. The melody that it all orchestrated in her heart always brought her back into the present moment.

She replayed the events of the past week, with shame rolling over her until she was nauseated again. She had not texted Holly or Lisa about losing her job, she felt that it was pointless as they would suggest drinking the pain away. She knew it was time to make serious changes in her life, as she could not go on like this.

She had seen a picture on Marias wall that said "Choose your Circle well." Hmm. Her circle was small, but seemed to be faulty. As much as she loved her friends, she realized that they were adding nothing positive or constructive to her life. She had met them in her senior year of high school, having taken Spanish together. They had hit it off immediately, but Danica had never made boundaries with either one of them.

It was good that she had met them the last year of high school as she had a 4.0 GPA until then. Her grandparents had been so proud of her grades. Holly and Lisa had such a talented way of coaxing Danica that she never told them no, even when she knew that she should. She knew her grandparents did not care for either girl. "You are going places Danica. You are such a bright star, your parents named you after the morning star. Don't let others dim your light," her granny had said.

Well, she had snuffed her light out, that was for sure. She pulled chips out of her back pack, tossing them to the seagulls. She loved the seagulls and their funny ways.

She thought of what her therapist had said of spirituality. Of course she believed in God, every one did. It was silly not to, she felt. There were too many daily synchronicities, too many everyday miracles, to negate something larger than us. That, though, was as far as her thoughts on spirituality went. Whenever she thought of going to church, however, fear would become so strong she would be nauseated.

Getting out her phone, she emailed Maria, asking to have an appointment as soon as possible. The last one had helped so much, perhaps Maria could tell her what to do next. It would be good to just have someone listen more.

Maria fit her in later that afternoon. Danica felt again, that she knew Maria from somewhere, but could not put her finger on where. She shared with Maria what happened the night before and then that morning. "I just don't know what to do with my life. Can you tell me what you think I should do?" she said, looking at Maria with the last bit of hope flickering in her eyes.

Maria felt for Danica. She too, had felt they knew each other from somewhere. Maria led a deeply spiritual life, she loved her creator deeply and connected daily. She believed in reincarnation and felt that they must have had some past life together, being close in that life. She felt they were meant to cross paths again, calling it the "Deja vu" of destiny.

"I cannot tell you what to do Danica, we are all on our own journeys. I believe you should find your path in your way. One way that helps the process is to take the time to see what you want out of life. I will give you some exercises to help with this by helping you to define what you want and not what others told you that you should have. For now, you should get to know Danica, really know her," Maria said.

She encouraged her to modify her habits, creating healthy boundaries with her friends. Maria explained what those healthy boundaries may look like. She sent Danica home with books to read to help her understand boundaries as well.

Those books from that office changed Danica's life. They awakened something that had been slumbering, her light. The first one she read from the moment that she got home until the wee hours of the morning.

It spoke of the importance of our feelings and our thoughts, how to decipher if they were our own or something that was taught or caught. "The only thing you can control are your feelings, so focus on feeling good", she read. Directing your thoughts, being aware of what you are thinking controls where your life is going, whether it will be positive or negative, was the summary she took away from the whole.

She had never thought of that, she felt like she had no control over anything. Her parents and grandparents death felt like proof of that. The more she read, though, the more that she had hope, perhaps she should start focusing on her inner dialogue more.

She joined a yoga class as well as a book club, introducing her to new, positive, friends. Even though she dearly loved Lisa and Holly, she made sure that she was busy every time that they wanted to hang out. She felt that if she were going to continue to get her life under control, partying every night was not going to do that. She had tried simply telling her friends this, but she realized they were just not in the same place in their life journey as she was.

She had not dated anyone since her grandparents passing. Before that she had dated Rick. When her grandparents passed, Rick could not handle the level of grief that Danica was experiencing. He told her that he felt that they needed to take a break. This led to Rick dating someone else, adding to Danica's grief.

Some people do not have the emotional or mental capacity to sit with us in out darkness. Often, this is all that we simply need, is for someone to hold space for us while we process. Danica felt relief that she had found this out before they had committed to each other, even though it still hurt. It had caused her to build a wall around her heart, feeling it was safer to be alone.

As she healed, she began to feel stirrings inside of her again. The desire to meet someone and connect. To find her person, as she called it.

She felt her life was beginning to fill with hope as she discovered more and more of who she was and how she believed. She was truly beginning to experience joy as she learned to live in the moment. She had scribbled in her journal that morning, "depression is from dwelling in the past, anxiety from dwelling in the future, but gratitude keeps us in the now," and she was learning how to live that.

Her weekly meetings with Maria as well as her changing life-style habits were showing on the outside of her as well. She began again to care about her appearance, not for anyone else's benefit but her own. She paid attention to what she ate and how it made her feel, leading to an increase in physical and mental energy.

Six months after her life began to change she told her friend Jenny that she had figured out what she wanted to do with her life. "I want to go to school to be a therapist. I want to help others the way that Maria has helped me."

She enrolled in her first semester of classes, deciding not to work as she went to school so that she could remain focused on the end goal. She still had much of what was left to her from her family passing. She sat, grateful that she had changed her life patterns before wasting all that had been given to her, now she did not have to feel overwhelmed by juggling so many things at once.

Holly and Lisa had faded out of her life all together. She had reached out to them periodically, inviting them to yoga as well as some of the other things that she had been learning and experiencing. When they did respond, it was to say they were too busy for that. Danica realized this was probably for the best, another lesson that all closed chapters are not a bad thing.

The first semester Danica kept her head down, determined to finish her classes in record time while keeping a high GPA. She often smiled to herself, thinking of how happy her family would be. In the evenings though, she began to feel herself get lonely.

There were a few nights that the temptation to repeat her old patterns would wash over her, because she felt the loneliness was too great to bear. Thankfully, she was learning better coping skills. She would call Jenny then, and they would go for a walk along the sea shore.

Maria loaned her a book as soon as Danica finished one. Being in college had slowed this down, but Danica was still able to read one a month. She was currently reading one on divination. Maria loved runes as her favorite form of divination, " I think it must be in my blood, everyone tells me that I read them like a book. I just seem to have a feeling, a knowing, of what each one is trying to say. To me it is so beautiful that it is such an old language that is still used today," she said to Danica one afternoon.

Runes are often some type of rock, crystal, wood or bone, with symbols on them. Each symbol has a different meaning, and many of them several different meanings. Maria had many different sets, made from different things.

Danica purchased a set for herself, Maria teaching her how to read and use them. "It's not that you are looking for the future. You are asking the universe, your higher self, your guides, your God, whatever you want to call it, how you are blocking yourself in life. You are looking to see what you need to shift, to see, to be a better you. They are a compass, a guidance system to help you connect to your divinity," Maria told her.

This made sense to Danica. If we are each accountable for our own soul, then we need to check on that soul daily. We need spirituality to still have spirit in it. We all like to ask, to tell God what to do, but we have forgotten how to listen.

Soon she had a morning routine that helped enhance the self discipline that she was learning. When she woke up in the morning she would do ten minutes of yoga. Afterwards she would get out her gratitude journal, taking a few minutes to write down everything that she was grateful for that morning.

Then she would get out her intention journal, taking a few minutes to write down what she would like to accomplish that day as well as how she would like her day to feel. She felt that this gave her a definite purpose and a clarity that she had not experienced before. It also gave her an idea of what areas she needed to ask the universe for help in.

Finally, she would get our her runes and do what Maria called "listening." "There is a whole universe waiting to help you, to guide you. You just have to remember to ask, but just as importantly, you have to learn how to listen. How to follow the little voice of intuition inside of you. This will take you places that otherwise you would have not gotten to," Maria had said.

The whole process only took Danica thirty minutes of her morning. She was learning that we have to take care of ourselves before we can take care of others. If we do not have a full cup to pour from, we can not add to others lives in a positive way.

The day came when Danica graduated from school. It had felt as if the last semester was going to last until she was elderly. She felt strong emotions as she received her diploma with honors, knowing that her family would be so proud of her.

Her friends threw her a graduation party and as she looked around the room at the friends that had become her family, she was grateful for rock bottom. That had propelled her to this moment of joy in her life. She was surrounded by people that loved and supported, people that she would not have met had she not had such adversity in her life.

She accepted a position as a therapist at an institute that provided therapy to those that came from lower socioeconomic backgrounds. Her grades had been such that she could have gotten a job anywhere, especially with her masters, but she wanted to give back to the community that had given so much to her.

She continued to see Maria once a month professionally, as she felt this was the best way to maintain while she continued to heal and grow. She had learned so much from Maria, she hoped to shine a light in someone's life the same way that Maria had done for her. This kept her inspired those first few weeks of working in a new environment.

During college Danica had pushed away her desire to date anyone, feeling that concentrating on school was a full time endeavor. Now she was beginning to have free time again, and it was crossing her mind more and more often. She had put it out into the universe, writing in her intention journal what she would like in a partner, and then leaving it in faith for the right one to show up.

She was about two weeks into her new job when she met another therapist. His name was Luke Evans, and once again, as with Maria, Danica had the strangest feeling that she knew him from somewhere. He had black hair, pulled back in a short pony tail, with brown eyes that were so dark they were almost black.

Danica was intrigued by the emotions that he brought out of her. On one hand her intuition was tingling, but not in a good way. She had been learning to follow that still, small voice inside. She and Jenny had attended several metaphysical classes on paying attention to how certain things make you feel. Whether it was what you were eating, where you were going, and especially who you had in your inner circle.

She had, though, such a strong sense of connection, of knowing him, that it seemed louder than her intuition that said, "let's just run along now."

When he came around she became giddy, embarrassing herself on s few occasions. "I don't know what it is about him. He feels like the terror of the sea, but at the same time, he feels like home," she told Jenny one afternoon.

Jenny had only met him once, but had not been impressed in a positive way. Her friends support helped her to giggle out her responses when Luke would ask her out. "I'm too busy tonight," or, "something else came up," were her go to responses. His face would light up with her giggles, and she would promptly retreat back to the safety of her office, feeling slightly ashamed that he had such an effect on her.

PART TWELVE

We are often not just one ingredient, but a mixture of sorts.
All that we have been through as well as the lack or gift of support.

Our origin is woven in our recipe of life.

Our formative years can reap peace or strife.

It is difficult to change, to alter the recipe late.

But here we are as humans, tossing it up to fate.

Luke had a very different upbringing than Danica. Her parents and grandparents had been very loving and supportive in so many different areas of her life. Their love was the legacy that they left her. It helped to mold her into the light that she was now.

Luke's parents, John and Cynthia, were part of a very strict religious group. He grew up with no T.V. or internet, with limited access to the world around him. Being home schooled made his world even smaller.

He had difficulty focusing, getting distracted easily from chores and tasks. Later on in life he learned that he had ADHD, which explained his difficulty focusing, but it did not save him in time from the beatings. His father believed he could fix Luke by beating the ornery out of him, as he would tell Cynthia when she would attempt to intercede.

This created a vicious cycle that absolutely no one won at. Luke's mother could see it as a cycle, but his father had his mind made up. "Luke will never amount to anything if we don't correct him," he would say.

So Cynthia would take a step back, allowing John to discipline, while she felt it was still so wrong. She understood her place in the home, though, and would not cross certain boundaries for fear of retribution form her God. She wanted the best for her son, she knew that she had to trust her husband for that wisdom.

As time went on, though, Cynthia could see the detrimental effects that the beatings were having on Luke. "Maybe we need to take him to a doctor and see if he has that ADHD," she told John.

"Absolutely not," John bellowed, "that's just the new definition of a generation of children that lack discipline."

Luke, however, seemed to be getting worse. He did have ADHD and was eventually diagnosed as an adult when he took himself. He struggled even then to take his medications, wondering off and on if he was all the things his father had spoken.

Reading this, it is easy to judge Luke's parents. Their reactions did shape who he was to become in a large measure, but that is all that they knew. When you take generational fear and mix it with religion, the reaction is often a volatile one.

Luke's grades struggled as his emotions spiraled. He would pick fights at school, coming home battered and bloody because he wouldn't back down. He always felt that he had something to prove. He did not realize until he was an adult that it was his self worth that he was trying to validate, since he had no positive validation in his home environment.

He ran away from home at sixteen. He had started to drink and smoke at fifteen. When his father found this out he gave him an ultimatum. Luke was done with ultimatum's, determined to live his life the way he saw fit.

These very real demons followed him through the rest of his teenage years and early adult life. Molding him as much as his parents did when he was younger. He lived for the next buzz, adding opioids to his dinner plans as well.

He had dropped out of high school, feeling that it was useless. Since he lived on his own he had to work , though, to pay his own bills. He created a toxic cycle through those years. Party hard, then miss work, then get fired, then start again.

His room mate Damien, told him one day that he would soon run out of places to work. Luke thought about that seriously, realizing that their was some fundamental truth in what he was saying. He felt it was time to get some help.

He remembered his mother talking about ADHD. Maybe that was why he was struggling so much. So he made an appointment with his doctor, and was diagnosed with ADHD and given the proper medication.

After he went home and read all of the teaching information about it that his doctor sent home with him, he became angry. He felt the resentment well up inside of him, that his father fought his mother in this area when he needed some very real help. He was angry at God, if there was a God, why would He let this happen to Luke? He didn't want to feel any of the emotions that were coursing through him, so he went home and drank, until he could not feel anything.

The following morning he was late to work, and lost his job, again. He also owed Damien two months rent. Damien gave him an ultimatum, get help, or move out. This angered Luke as he still did not feel that he had a problem. In fact, he was the victim in this circumstance, loosing his job and all.

He didn't want to be homeless though, or worse, ask his parents for help, so he started attending a weekly meeting with others that were recovering from addictions. This became a pivotal point in his life.

Hearing their stories as well as the ability to be open in a safe environment put a new determination in Luke's heart for life. It made him finally decide what he wanted to be "when he grew up." He felt a therapist was the best line of work to help make the change in others lives that he had felt in his own.

He applied for college after taking his GED. He entered into it whole heartedly, making the deans list every semester. During this time he and Cynthia became closer while the gap with his father grew. It was not for a lack of Luke trying, or Cynthia for that matter.

John never apologized or backed down from his original thought that Luke just needed more discipline. It had caused a rift between he and Cynthia, and John blamed Luke for this. John would mutter that he should have beaten more of it out of Luke so that he would not use it as an excuse to take drugs, even though they were prescribed.

Cynthia pointed out how that since the medication Luke was able to focus more, making the deans list every semester. John would remark then that it was from the prayers and discipline that Luke had received, not the medication. Cynthia dare not push too hard because of the retribution that it may bring to her. She loved Luke dearly, but she still lived with John.

Once Luke finished school he applied for a job. Because his history of work was so negative, this proved to be more difficult than what he had imagined. His underlying dream to work at a prestigious facility to once again prove his worth to his parents, was all but gone.

He finally applied at a facility that was located in what he considered the slums, and was accepted. He felt that if he could get his foot in the door somewhere, he could move his way up the ladder. He felt confident that he would only have to stay in this position for a short period before he moved on to something that would prove his worth to his parents.

He had also recently started dating a girl. They had met at the group meetings that he attended for his alcohol addiction. It seemed to be going well, he felt that way at least. Though they didn't have much in common other than a problem with addiction, but Luke felt that would change as they healed together.

Her name was Terry, that was the extent of the information that he gave to Cynthia. The relationship was very short-lived. What Terry did do for Luke was introduce him back to his old friend, beer and liquor. "One drink wont hurt," she said, "we have better self control than that."

One drink then turned into a fifth of whiskey, and Luke was late for work. As this was obviously Terry's fault, Luke ended the relationship with her. He did, however, continue his relationship with alcohol.

He knew that he would have to be smarter about his drinking or he would once again lose his job, he couldn't afford that. Not only financially, but with his parents. And he could not climb the ladder of success that he had planned if he were fired from the bottom rung, possibly loosing his license.

So he learned to pace himself. I believe the correct terminology is functioning alcoholic. He made peace with himself that during the work week he would only drink four or five drinks after work. The weekend, well, that was different. From Friday when he clocked out until late Sunday afternoon, he was drunk.

He had the occasional morning toddy during the week day if he had drank a little too much. He learned this help curve the hangover until he got home and could drink more. He felt this was the secret that he had been missing before.

He did not realize that the other therapists had smelled alcohol on him several times. No one was brave enough to confront him, but they all made mental notes. Hence his reputation was painted as " hot bad boy." His motorcycle just added to that definition.

He had been working in the "slums" for about a year when he met a young woman in the hallway. She had honey brown hair with pale blue eyes. She seemed to light up the space that they were in. He stuck out his hand to meet her in mid stride, almost falling against the wall.

When their eyes met, he felt strongly that he knew her. "Have I met you some where before, it feels as if I have." Luke told her.

She had felt that way also, but only commented that they had not met. She shared that her name was Danica, that she was excited to work there and give back to the community. He smiled while shaking her hand, making a mental note immediately that she was a tree hugger.

It seems that for some of the human population we have genetically carried a caste system in our minds. If we are not mindful of our thoughts we tend to put people there almost effortlessly. Sometimes never giving them the opportunity to share with us who they truly are.

Luke could not shake his attraction to her, or the feeling that he knew her, so he asked her out. He waited a few weeks before doing so, noting her slight aversion of him. He had wondered if she had heard of his track record of drinking from their coworkers.

Danica had not heard anything about Luke from coworkers, but she was learning to follow her intuition, and how things made her feel. When Luke was near all of her warning bells went off like a wedding at a cathedral. She felt that this should be taken into consideration.

She, also, could not shake the fact that she knew him from somewhere, though. Whenever they would pass in the hall and he would speak, she would blush. Emotions would rush to the surface of her being that should not be there. The only thing that she knew about this man was what her gut was telling her. Nevertheless, after a few weeks of giggling in the hall, when he asked her to dinner she said yes.

PART THIRTEEN

In the corners of my mind,

in the realms deep within my soul,

I feel that I must know you,

that you must be part of what makes me whole.

Somewhere we must have walked together,

another life, another time.

Somewhere we danced together,

because it feels that you are already mine.

In some ethereal plane, our fates have crossed before.

So in this life as others, I will get to know you more, as mine.

Luke was so happy that morning that he hadn't needed a morning toddy. He was getting better about pacing himself after work, resulting in less hangovers the following day. He also had a date with Danica that night, he was dreaming about it while he got ready for work. So far his favorite thing about her was her laugh, it felt contagious, and he was planning on hearing more of it.

Work was a little awkward that day for both of them, as they didn't want anyone they worked with finding out that they had a date. They had different reasons for this. Luke didn't want to close off his options at the office if this didn't work out. Danica still had this gut feeling that was growing louder.

Danica had stopped seeing Maria professionally as their friendship had grown. She had shared her excitement about her date and then Maria asked to see his picture. Maria had this strange, unpleasant feeling that she knew Luke from somewhere, and wherever that was, it was not a good place.

She felt that she could not alter Danica's plans on an assumption of feeling so she tried to feel excitement for her young friend. When they parted ways, Maria went home, spreading her rune cloth out, and asked her guides what this feeling meant. She was not surprised by the answer that she received.

Maria believed in reincarnation, she called it the wheel of life. She had learned that when she felt as if she knew someone, but had never met them in this life, that they had shared a previous life together. She had also learned though out her life that running into these people was not a coincidence, but usually something that needed to be worked out from the previous life that they had.

The runes told the story of how she, Danica and Luke had all had a life together. From what she could divine, she and Danica had been friends in that life as well, but she and Luke had been strained, and she had seen abuse as well. That explained the feelings that she felt when she saw his picture.

She went on to read that it would play out the way that it needed to in this life, that she should not interfere as healing needed to happen. She felt that the universe was her friend, she respected it's advice. She would not interfere but would pray for Danica's safety and protection. She would be there for her.

Luke chose the swankiest restaurant that Beaufort had. He opened doors and pulled out chairs for Danica to sit in, his charm turned on to maximum southern. Danica took note of all this, telling her gut it was wrong. The evening flew by as they had so much in common and felt the same on many different subjects. The conversation was connecting and stimulating to both of them. Luke took Danica home, kissing her good night and telling her that he would see her at work tomorrow.

Danica lay in bed, joy in her heart, such a joy that she had not felt since baking with her grandmother. "I know it sounds cheesy, but he feels like home," she told Jenny, who agreed with the cheesy part, but was happy for her friend.

"What do you know about him Danny? Good feels are great, but knowing all the pages of his story are even better," Jenny said.

Danica thought about Jenny's words. What did she know about him? He was handsome, her mind trailed away on that one for a moment. From what she had seen he was an excellent therapist.

He saw mainly teenagers, she had seen him interacting with them in the hallway several times. She had been impressed by the way that he could make them feel at ease, lowering their emotional walls. She knew from experience that was a gift.

"They come through the door, terrified of judgement, stuck in flight or fight. They are unwilling to share their trauma with anyone, but he has a way of disarming them, of making them feel safe," she said to Jenny.

Jenny had just brought to Danica her concern again that there were no walls left between she and Luke. "You have to get to know him better Danny, I don't want to see you get hurt, you are a good person, deserving of the best."

Danica had to admit to herself that she really did not know that much about Luke. She knew his parents were still alive because he had mentioned them. She knew where he worked because she worked there also, and that was the end of her list. Her gut was still giving her that nudge to run, but she was getting better at ignoring it.

They went on a few more dates before Danica shared what she had been through, how therapy had helped her, leading her here. Luke listened, nodding here and there in the appropriate places, telling her how he glad he was that she had gotten help. Danica, with naivety, took that response to mean that he was, in fact, a good person, her gut had been wrong and she had been right to ignore it.

She looked up, meeting his eyes, and her heart did a little dance in her chest. That was the first night that he stayed over at her house. She woke up nestled in his arms, grateful that she was no longer alone.

Danica could not stop smiling at work the next day. This annoyed Luke slightly as he did not want anyone else at work to know what was going on. He kept his distance from Danica for the day, even ignoring her texts. He liked Danica, a lot, but their values were so different.

She was always seeing the cup half full, that was annoying to him, life just wasn't like that. When she told him that she chose to work in the slums, that had shocked him as well. He did not want to stay on the lowest part of the totem pole, especially with how little pay they received for the responsibilities that they had. He could not, however, shake the connection that he felt for her, making him more testy.

Halfway through the day Danica caught on that Luke was ignoring her. This confused her, as well as hurt her since they had just spent the night together. She had felt so sure snuggled up to him, of his feelings for her.

This lasted for two weeks before Jenny noticed that Danica was loosing weight. She quizzed her friend on her life, becoming upset when Danica shared what was going on between herself and Luke. "I feel such a connection when we are together. The emotional confusion has been a bit much for me, though. I am struggling to sleep at night, food doesn't have the same taste, and Jenny I am truly ashamed that I contemplated drinking a beer the other day as well."

"Danny, this is not normal behavior. He obviously does not want a relationship, only to hook up. This could take your life down a path that you don't want, and definitely don't need," Jenny said.

Danica knew that her friend was right, she did not want to continue this way. She called into work sick the next few days while she figured out what she wanted in life. Maria had told her repeatedly, "The Lord doesn't know what to bless you with if you don't know what you want yourself. That's life lesson number one, what do you want in life? What do you want in this moment?"

Danica knew she did not want the feelings that were going through her now. She could see that Jenny was right, if she continued on this trajectory she would be right back where she was several years ago. Most of our battles are in the decision making themselves. Often we have relief simply from clarity, even though the clarity made Danica cry.

She got out her runes, casting them the way that Maria had taught her. She felt the presence of angels while she prayed for strength to not grieve over it all with a bottle in her hand. She practiced the coping mechanisms that she now taught to others, while continuing to process all of her emotions.

Grief was the word of the day as she had felt something with Luke that she had never felt with anyone else. She felt like she was bigger, somehow, around him. As if her soul was bigger.

She had only told Maria about the depth of her feelings, as she didn't want to sound any crazier than it all already looked. Maria, having put it all together, hugged her, saying, "We all have many lives, many journeys. Some individuals walk through lives with us more often than others."

Danica thought of those words as she pieced together what the runes were saying: that the best route she could take at the moment was to keep the relationship with Luke professional at this time. She sighed as tears trickled down her face. It was a sigh of sadness as well as relief, to have made a final decision.

On her last day of self care she texted Luke, replying to the repeated text of "what are you doing later tonight?" She sent back, "I think it's best if we keep everything professional."

Luke felt as if someone had punched him in the stomach. He had not expected, or wanted that reply. He realized just how much he enjoyed Danica's company. Not just the physical aspects of it, but her sense of humor and intelligence as well.

And her laugh. You felt like the world must be laughing with her, in a positive way. Her smile lit up the room.

Luke began to be aware of his thoughts and where they were headed in this. It was one girl, he shouldn't let it bother him like this. He texted back, "if you change your mind, let me know."

There was no reply, this angered him. He was home for the day so he poured a drink, that led to a fifth of whiskey later. He reasoned within himself that he would stop as soon as he could not feel the anger any longer.

He woke up on the floor, by his couch, to his morning alarm. Potato chips were littered around his body as if he had tried to baste himself in them. His podcast from the previous day was still playing. He tried moving, the potato chips inside of him exiting rapidly.

He refused to call in as that would be obvious to Danica of how he felt. He frowned at the mixture of feelings she brought to his mind and body. This was her fault, him regressing like this.

It had not occurred to Luke yet that he had created all of this, as his mind still blamed everyone else in its path, especially those closest to him. He had begun to notice though, thanks to his line of work, his tendency to have a victim mentality. He had found that if he stated out loud the reality of the situation versus his perception of it that the brain fog he experienced when he was triggered and responded from a place of trauma would lift, and he could see the whole of the truth associated with it. As he had gotten better at being a functioning alcoholic, though, his thought patterns as well as good habits that he had learned, were struggling from it.

He pulled himself together, going to work, acknowledging Danica on a professional level. The day was not an easy one, pushing him to look at job openings elsewhere. He had known when he took this job it was the bottom of the totem pole, it was just time to climb higher, he thought.

A job listing caught his eye, he recognized the name. It was a manny position for one of the wealthiest families in Beaufort. It was not something that he would have ever imagined doing, but he applied any way.

When he went for his interview he was shocked by the amount of money that they were offering. He had only even considered applying because their name on a resume in any capacity would help him move more towards where he wanted to be. His current boss was kind enough to write him a letter of recommendation.

He did not know that he could be so nervous for anything. He rebuked himself for being so childish. These were just people, like he was, he told himself.

The door opened to the sitting room that he was waiting in and a pleasant looking woman came in. Luke knew from the family photos that she must have been one of the staff as she wasn't in any of the photos. He had done some homework before his interview.

She escorted him to another part of the house. It was decorated in a resonance theme, with massive doorways and wide fireplaces in every room. He couldn't help but think that the family would be just fine in an apocalypse.

Luke had only been seated a moment when a short, balding man came in and shook his hand. Luke had read that Simon Bruster was short, but nothing on how pale he was. Pasty, like glue, was more of the description that Luke would go with. Luke had that Deja vu feeling again, that they had met before. He shrugged it off as a recognition from all the publicity the family received locally.

Simon began the conversation by saying that he had heard how well Luke interacted with teenagers. The job would require him to take care of their ten year old autistic son Sean. He would be helping him at school as well as his other activities such as tennis, golf and musical lessons.

Luke knew that he wanted the job, but wanting to seem professional he told Simon that he needed a few days to think about the offer. He accepted it, turning in his notice at his current job. He felt like his life was finally headed in the right direction.

He acknowledged Danica professionally, keeping a wall around his emotions. Danica, on the other hand, was a bit of a mess. She could not just shut her feelings off for him. Work that had once been exciting and rewarding seemed to drag out in a very painful way.

They were both relieved when his last day of work came. They were cordial throughout the day as well as the farewell party. That night Danica wrestled with herself, tempted to drink the pain away. She knew that one drink would lead to another.

She got out her runes, asking for direction and comfort from the guides that had become her friends as well. Her rune spread told the tale of new beginnings, ending cycles, and Danica's favorite part, hope. They gave her hope that tomorrow would not hurt this much. Then the following day would be better, until there was no longer the echoing pain that now resided inside of her chest cavity. She thanked the universe for it's love and guidance, and then crept into bed, tears covering her pillow.

PART FOURTEEN

I knew you were there,
somewhere there,
in the corners of my mind.
Time, distance, education,
my mind is crowded,
but there you still lie.
Tucked away in memories,

that still feel so very real.
Tucked away in emotions,

though it's not ideal.
On quiet days when I am still,
I can hear the beat of your heart.
Closing my eyes I see your face,

a gift memory imparts.
I almost feel with all I am,

the touch of your hand.
Feeling again, not so lost,

in the life that we had planned.
I'll walk with my memories,

emotions greater than fear.
As they climb to the top of my mind,
rolling out through my tears.

Ten years had passed since that night the universe told Danica that the pain would fade. She had a beautiful daughter in that span of time, named Phoebe. She was in the middle of divorcing Phoebes father, not sure how they had married in the first place, looking back. Maria had muttered through the years of rebound love, but never loud enough for Danica to hear.

She was able to keep the family home thanks to following Marias intuition before the wedding. When Maria had first brought up a prenuptial agreement it had hurt Danica's feelings. She had replied that she trusted her future husband or she would not have married him. But she had seen that Maria was usually on point with her guidance system, so she grumpily agreed. It turned out to be a good thing that she did, as he fought her tooth and nail for all that they owned.

When they had met, he owned nothing but some clothes. He had been quick to claim everything about Danica as his own, including what she owned. Danica thought that since he was open about their relationship it was much better than Luke who had wanted to hide it. She had felt and seen all the red flags, but pushed them over and walked past.

Maria had felt that the relationship had been built on Danica trying to forget Luke. She had seen her friend ignore the red flags, even waving some. She knew that all she could do was stand by her and wait.

Danica split custody with Phoebe's father so that neither would have to pay child support. He would not have been able to pay it, as money sifted through his fingers like sand. He was a good father, though, and Danica was very grateful for this.

She had opened her own office two years previously and was doing very well. She felt that she was on a good trajectory. Her divorce had actually added a positive aspect to her life as the last six months of their marriage were as Maria said, "Very low vibe."

She and Phoebe spent as many weekends as the weather let them at the ocean. At four Phoebe enjoyed building sand castles but found the real joy in tearing them down. Danica was so happy and content that when Maria asked her about dating again she replied, "Phoebe and I are doing great as we are, men complicate things."

Maria wondered if it weren't more likely that Danica had never been able to replicate that feeling of connectedness that she had with Luke. Once that is felt it is difficult to go back to mediocracy. Once your soul recognizes another soul at that magnitude, it starts a little fire inside, a fire that does not burn out easily. Our lives are much like tapestries in that we weave in and out with those that we have such a connection with and Danica would experience this more.

She was at a restaurant with Phoebe six months after her divorce, when she heard her name called by a voice that she had only heard in her memories. She felt her heart catch in her throat as she looked up, meeting Luke's eyes. She had not seen him since he had quit, all those years ago.

"Mommy your face is red," she heard Phoebe say.

Ugh, it was, she could feel it creeping up from her neck. She caught herself, regaining her emotions as well as composure. She motioned with her hand for Luke to take a seat with them. She introduced him to Phoebe, who went right back to eating. His face lit up with the introduction as he said, " She looks like your mini me."

They caught up on their work lives, Luke sharing that he was still with the Brusters as Sean could not function without assistance. He explained how it had opened the door for him to work with other autistic children as well. He ended his story with his divorce story. "Lasted two years and she was an absolute sea witch."

Danica, in turn, shared her story of divorce as well as starting her own practice. She answered his questions about Phoebe that he did not direct at Phoebe himself. There were no awkward silences as time slipped away swiftly. Even in the brief silences they still felt as if they could hear each other.

He came home with her, sitting on the couch while she put Phoebe to bed. He put a movie on to watch and Danica snuggled in to him, where the world felt right, once more. She didn't know why, only that it did.

The next morning Luke was humming at work. Sean made a comment about his happiness. Luke replied with a cheesy smiled that he was happy.

Danica covered Phoebes face in kisses when she woke her up, sending her into a volley of giggles. She scooped her up, twirling her, humming a song. She could not remember the last time that she had felt this happy. The day passed swiftly and that night Luke brought dinner to the house as well as a bottle of wine.

Throughout the years Luke had managed to keep up with being a functioning alcoholic while keeping his outside appearances up. It was, in part, what ruined his marriage. He was a lovable drinker when the night was young, but after so many shot glasses he became mean, angry, and a tad bit violent.

He had never hit anyone, but his aggression was over powering and definitely not enjoyable to be around. Luke felt that his ex had antagonized him to that point, which was partially true. But it was more that she was exhausted from dealing with that side of him daily, she wanted to be free of her nightly baby sitting duties.

When Luke set the table he poured himself and Danica a glass of wine. Danica smiled, her eyes full of light, "Thank you, but I do not drink, especially not with Phoebe here."

He tried to playfully argue with her, but Danica would not be moved on that subject. He let the subject drop, not wanting to spoil a nice evening. One bottle of wine was a simple appetizer for him, and Danica was so into her feelings that she did not notice with what minimal effort said bottle disappeared with. They watched comedy shows and discussed what empires that they wanted to build, what difference that they wanted to make.

And so the days were full of hope and connection once more. Even though it was already there, unbeknown to Luke and Danica, they became full of love for each other. Their joy in love touched everyone that they met, so strong was the emotion.

Danica did not have Phoebe on the weekends so she began to stay at Luke's apartment. They watched movies, played games, listened to music, and laughed, so much. It was if their inner children came out, and they played well together. For both of them it was some of the most enjoyable time that they had spent as adults.

"They have this uncanny ability to almost finish the other one's thoughts. When you are with them you can feel the connection," Jenny told Maria after a month of watching the couple interact.

Maria remembered what she had learned of the couple, she knew there was a deep connection. With that in mind she coaxed Danica into doing a past life session with a healer that she thought highly of. She explained to Danica how she would be hypnotized, remembering events from previous lives.

Danica meditated daily, keeping a journal of all that she felt the universe told her in her daily morning ritual. She listened to Maria intently, feeling that this would only add to her spiritual journey. She agreed and they made the appointment.

She told Luke all about it, he smiled, listening. He was agnostic, however he enjoyed watching Danica light up whenever she shared what she had learned in her morning mediations. He was impressed with her ability to read runes. While she explained the appointment he nodded while pouring a little beer in her empty water glass.

He had been giving her small amounts of alcohol here and there. Much like water wears away at rock he had worked at it diligently. He felt the key was to not let her notice, then she would not struggle with guilt. He did not like to drink alone.

He had managed to keep it from his employer all of these years. When he and Danica first started dating again he had kept it from her as well, at least the actual amount of what he drank. She wondered later if his lack of wanting to drink alone was more to appease his conscious because of the sheer amount of alcohol that he actually consumed.

At first she had continually pushed his hand away when it had alcohol in it. So he became craftier. "Taste this babe, I want to see what you think," he started to say when pushing the glass toward her.

That seemed harmless enough to Danica as it was such a small amount. It had been so many years, surely she had more self control than she had then. They would put music on, play the guitar, and dance the night away.

Some nights Luke would read her poetry from the large library of books that he had. Danica would become wrapped up in the words as well as the intonation of his voice as he poured his slightly intoxicated heart into it. And they were happy.

Danica was a little buzzed that Saturday night when Luke scooped her up, "You are going to be hypnotized soon, I have to get my time in before your feelings are hypnotized away."

He was only half joking as he carried her to bed. He was so happy, but he had a worry in the back of his head that it would all disappear. Fear, as it often does, likes to grab anything in our life by the hand and say, "Look at this, it can't be safe." I have found it is best to name your fear, mine is named Alice. That way you can call it by name as you tell it that you will have none of those thoughts. Luke had not learned this yet, instead having extra stomach acid with headaches from walking with his fear.

Danica had a slight headache the next morning. She mentally reproved herself for not drinking more water. She was a little ashamed of herself that she had allowed herself to drink as much alcohol as

she did. Oh well, she would be more careful next time. She smiled at the memory of the previous night, especially Luke carrying her to bed.

Her appointment was after work at a metaphysical store that following Monday. Even though Maria was a friend of the practitioner, Danica had never met her, making her a little nervous. "What if I can't be hypnotized?" she asked Maria.

Maria encouraged her that it was not like what she had seen on T.V., telling her to record it so that she could go back to it later. Maria went with her, reading a book while she waited after she introduced them to each other. The woman that opened the door after hours was short, Danica didn't think she was even five foot, with brown hair, and brown eyes. Some may have called her plain looking if it weren't for her eyes, they were full of life and fire.

She took Danica by the hand and led her into a quiet room in the back of the store, introducing herself as Yolanda. Danica thought of a few horror memories that started this way, but then silenced her inner dialog before it could talk her out of going through with the hypnotism. Yolanda asked her a few questions before she had her lay down and silence her phone.

Yolanda took Danica through a process of suggestive thoughts, Danica falling under to the words while her past life memories came back. And she remembered. She remembered being Sara, then the morning star, and finally, Luece. She remembered Luke as Samiel, and then Hades. She remembered Maria when she was the Oracle for Hades, seeing how their friendship had just carried into their next life.

She recognized Simon Bruster as Osephus, giggling in the middle of her session as she realized the karma that Luke was working through. She felt such joy as the memories and emotions poured through. The feeling of being an angel and creating, followed by the morning star, leading those pilgrims through the dark. The feeling of Samiel, Hades now turned Luke and she smiled with that love.

The session ended as the tears of relief and wonder rolled down her face. She hugged Yolanda, sincerely thanking her. Danica could not wait to get home and play the recording for Maria.

The babysitter had put Phoebe to bed, so they listened to it right away. "No wonder I love my cats," Maria said, " sounds like I had something similar in the underworld."

Maria then shared with Danica what she had seen so many years ago. She explained that she felt it would sound crazy if Danica did not figure it our for herself. "It all makes sense now why we all felt as if we knew each other! Because we did," Danica said, followed by a yawn.

Maria hugged her good night, hoping that her friend would see all sides of Luke equally. Hades was a well known character in history, and it wasn't for being a good Samaritan. Maria did not want to see Luke dim Danica's bright light. With knowledge comes power, and Danica was smart enough to use this power wisely. She was earnestly praying that in playing the recording for Luke he would remember also.

It was the following Friday night and she had dropped Phoebe off a little earlier than normal at her dads so that they had time to listen and process the whole weekend. When she got to Luke's he was a little more than buzzed. His sloppy kiss was evidence of his slowing reflex's due to his already high alcohol content.

She paused, she didn't want him to listen like this, that was for sure. She felt some pity as she remembered all the addictions that Hades had accumulated throughout his lifetime. Luke could definitely be worse.

He was pouring her a glass of some mixture that he had made. She felt that she should probably say no, but she wanted to celebrate with him. And from that point on the weekend was foggy.

She missed picking Phoebe up on time from her ex husband. She was so sick Monday morning that she had to cancel her clients for the day. She lay in the fetal position on the bathroom floor as the waves of nausea rolled over her and her head threatened to explode from her body. What was she thinking? Luke's only reply was to text her back that she was a light weight, with a winkie face.

She was torn inside over the knowledge that she had acquired, their lives together, the memories that had flooded her. Once the room stopped spinning she was able to think a little clearer. She knew that she needed more help processing it all, so she went to Maria. Sweet Maria, ever the Oracle in all of her lives. How incredible to have such a connection not only in one life, but multiple, Danica thought.

Maria listened to Danica's tale of the weekend, noting that the hypnosis only made Danica further ignore some bright red flags with Luke. She listened as Danica went on about fate and destiny. Maria felt that the conversation was needing to be brought to the point at hand so she said, "So Luke was an addict much like Hades?"

That silenced Danica's chatter as the truth hit her. She realized the layers of trauma that he had. She began to question her own sanity.

"I, as your friend, want you to be aware of the reality that you are walking. You missed picking up Phoebe as well as work, that is unlike you, and that is your current reality," Maria said.

No amount of arguing over fate versus destiny would have snapped Danica back where she needed to be as that comment did. The truth of it stung, but Danica knew that she needed to hear it. What was she doing? What was she thinking?

Luke was in many ways worse than he was as Hades, especially since he lost the knowledge of where he had come form, and who he had been . Perhaps that was karma for the atrocities that he had committed as Hades, they may never know. She knew that Simon Bruster had been Osephus, and from what she understood of karma, Luke was atoning for how he had treated Osephus when he was Hades.

She smiled at the memory of Osephus and Dahlia. She sat a little straighter wondering if Luanne, Simons wife, could be Dahlia. She realized that chance was fairly slim, though.

Danica shook her head, asking Maria if she thought that the alcohol had killed off more brain cells than expected. Maria smiled and said, "No, but you can't get caught up in what was, you have to walk in what is."

Danica looked at the patterns that were evolving in her life over the past few months. She did not like the totality of what she was seeing. Why couldn't life be simpler?

When she was with Luke the world just felt different. Jenny had laughed at her over this, calling her cheesy, but Danica felt it to be the truth. The weekends together were a world in their own. She had not remembered such joy in this life. But when she looked at where she was headed with drinking the magic was zapped right out of the emotions.

Friday night Danica shared with Luke her struggle with alcohol after her grandparents death. She told him of how she had lost her job, feeling so low that suicide made sense. "I don't want to mix that feeling with the feelings that I have for you," she said.

Luke, who was already buzzed, told her that the trick she was missing was to pace herself and hydrate. He also gave away just how addicted he was when he said, "That way when you start in the morning you can go all day."

Danica was quiet, she was trying to remember him as Hades, but other than during hypnosis, she could not bring memories up to the front of her head. She made a mental note to schedule another session. She playfully pushed the drink aside, convincing Luke to drop the subject by playing a movie that he had wanted to see.

On Saturday night they went out for dinner. Danica was exhausted from continually explaining why she did not want a drink. She had finally let him pour them, and then just left them on the table. He would forget that he had poured them for her and would drink them himself. She admitted to herself that this was not as magical an experience sober.

They were waiting in line to get into a club when Luke bumped into a large, stocky man. The woman standing with him whipped around saying, "You best get your man out of here, before my man kills his drunk ass."

Danica drug Luke away, her stomach growling. Luke was so intoxicated that he fell in the road in front of the restaurant. Danica, face red with embarrassment, helped him to his feet, and he immediately walked to a tree line. It was too late to stop him when she realized what he was doing as he unzipped his pants, urinating on a tree.

Danica was furious with Luke. She loved him, truly she did with a connection that she had never felt with anyone else before. But Maria was right, it was not about what was, it was about what is. This behavior, this would not be her life, no matter what the other lives had been.

She coaxed him into her car to drive them home. He tried giving her directions and she ignored him. So he repeated them louder. When Danica ignored him the second time it angered him leading to an explosion of foul language and hate.

Tears trickled down Danica's face as she pulled into his driveway. She ran in to get her things as Luke screamed, " Get out of my house, you senseless woman, you cant even follow directions."

Danica cried herself to sleep that night. Sunday morning Luke woke up, reaching for Danica. She was not on her side of the bed. Ugh, his head was pounding, he had not felt this bad in awhile. He gulped a bottle of water, then a beer, trying to appease his hangover.

He was trying to remember what had happened the night before. He checked the time, it was noon already, so he tried calling her. No answer. His gut flopped around. What had he done, or said?

It took a few hours for his head to cooperate with the rest of his body to drive, he had a second beer as he felt he could drive with alcohol in his system, but not a hangover. This was a huge misconception that he had created to validate his addiction. He drove to Danica's house where he found her car gone. Because he could not remember anything he did not have the courage to go looking for her. He felt that she was most likely at Jenny or Maria's, and he did not care for either one of them, especially Maria, it felt like she was looking into his soul and knew all of his secrets.

He went home, trying to call Danica one more time before he went back to his good friends whiskey and vodka. Because of his increasing incidences as the night before, he did not have too many actual friends left. His last waking thought was, "I hope I did not push Danica away the way that I have others."

PART FIFTEEN

There are moments in our life, decisions to be made,

that impact our future, they set forth a wave.

A ripple in time that we are unaware,

so make each decision with deep thought and care.

For it will steer who you are from where you have been.

It will make you or break you, the failure or win.

So take just a moment, a breath in and out,

as you follow your intuition through your mental doubt,

and create a life of joy, of peace;

from the positive decisions that you took the time to release.

Danica had texted Luke the next morning that she needed space after the weekend events. Luke apologized and Danica replied with, "Though I appreciate your apology, this is becoming an increasing problem, and I want my life to equal more than an apology."

Luke respected what she was saying, though it made him angry. He felt that she should cut him more slack as he was genuinely sorry and was working to cut back. When she mentioned that he should get help he was done with the conversation as well as her for that moment.

Tears rolled down Danica's face as she made Phoebe's supper. A few more slipped out when Phoebe asked where Luke was as he usually came for dinner. She explained to her small daughter that Luke had some things that he had to do before he could come over again, this seemed to satisfy the little girl.

When Danica went to bed she tucked pillows all around her. If she pretended that he was there, maybe it wouldn't hurt so much. She knew that she was going to have to make a serious decision. She loved Luke, loved their connection and time together, but not how the last while was going.

She thought of him, perched on the edge of his sofa, his glasses sliding down the end of his nose as he read poetry to her. He loved the arts, good writing, beautiful paintings, and music. He loved all genre of music, saying that there was a song for every mood, every day, every need. She appreciated his multifaceted personality.

She knew, if nothing else from her job, that an addiction like his was and would be the monster in the room. Every one wondering when it would rear its head, destroying all that the human being loved, without the human being remembering, or knowing what they had done. Tearing their life apart with a brutal force of need and desire.

Danica shuddered under her covers, realizing that could have been her just as well. She was grateful as she pondered her daughter and office, realizing one wrong drink could have taken that away, or made it never exist in the first place. She fell asleep with a prayer for clarity on her heart.

Luke and Danica did not communicate with each other for several days. Danica was waiting for clear direction from the universe before she reached back out to Luke. Luke was angry, and growing more angry that Danica did not simply accept his apology, after all mistakes happen.

Luke loved Danica dearly, but he loved his ego just a little more. He didn't want to change. It wasn't as if he got black out drunk all that often. He could not see that he had done it enough to systematically lose all of his friends. He was worried that Danica was going to make it some sort of requirement for their relationship that he go get help and this irritated him as well.

He could help himself, he knew how to pace himself. Alcohol was good for you, he felt that he had learned that at church even, when Jesus turned water into wine. He felt that was a definite sign that it was good and holy.

He had recently told Danica that he was tired of living in Beaufort. He had wanted to date her a little longer though to see if they could leave together. He felt in his heart that he could not leave her. He paced his apartment as all of these thoughts raced through his head.

She had said that she needed space to process, but what did that look like? His own personal guilt was lessoning as the days slipped by, and it was becoming more difficult for him to be patient. Especially since he could not remember what happened. He felt that this space thing should be over already.

He missed Danica but did not want to be the one to break the silence, it was her turn to apologize. With that thought he opened his laptop on a whim, looking for jobs out of state. He wanted to move to Franklin Tennessee, it was close to Nashville, and he felt this would be a positive change for his career since he had been a manny for over a decade.

The Brusters paid him well, but he had felt the whole time that Simon never really cared for him. Had you asked Mr. Bruster he would have answered that Luke was very good with Sean, but there was something that he just couldn't put his finger on (we have a pretty good idea as to why though, don't we my friend). Sometimes when Luke passed him in the hall he would shudder.

At first his father had been impressed by the amount of money he was making, but this wore off and John would make snide remarks about his son the manny. He brought it up at holidays and family gatherings. This took the joy out of the job eventually for Luke all together.

Luke pulled up job openings in Franklin, three popping up right away. All three were for positions asking for a degree that he held. One was a very prominent office that he could move up in.

Nashville had so many fun things to offer, especially in the line of entertainment. No small sleepy town there. In that moment he felt that he could not get away from Beaufort fast enough so he applied for all three. He was holding out hope that he would get the one in the prominent office.

Since Danica wasn't there to help him pace himself he spent the weekend drinking heavily while listening to music. He could not have told you on Monday what he had done, but he felt that it was a good time. He felt a small amount of concern that he had blacked out two weekends in a row, but brushed it off as his grieving process with Danica.

Danica spent the weekend tearfully searching her soul, asking through her tools of divination for direction. She thought of when Maria had her first start to take classes on the different means of divination and connecting to source. "Are you sure Maria that this is not evil, isn't better if you ask a minister these hard questions?" she had asked with concern.

Maria had hugged her, telling her that we are all divine, each one of us. That there was nothing evil about connecting to that divinity. "You don't need someone else to connect you to your creator for you. If you wanted to talk to Jenny, would you hand me the phone? No. you would call her yourself. You just have to remove the guilt, fear and shame that block you from seeing and feeling that connection."

Danica started to see an energy healer after that, to help her clear the trauma that she held inside of her. "We are all energy, that energy is in continual movement and it is our responsibility to keep that energy clear to move," Maria had said.

Danica would sit up after a session, feeling lighter when it was over. As time went on she noticed a different feeling afterwards. It was strange at first, a new sensation, then she realized that it was joy, pure joy.

Having learned all of these things helped her maneuver through the feelings that she was currently experiencing with Luke. She was grateful that they did not still work together as they did those years ago. She needed this space to juggle her head and her heart, and understand her own needs.

It was Wednesday when Luke heard back from two of the three jobs that he applied for, one of them being the one that he had so wanted. They set up a time to do a virtual interview the following day, and Luke felt good about it when it was over. They had a second interview the following week, offering him the job.

It had been several weeks since Danica had asked for space, Luke felt that should have been plenty of time for her to be resentful, or whatever it was that women do during the space that they ask for. Luke was so excited about his new job and getting away from the town that he hated, as well as proving himself to his parents, finally. He wanted to share all of this with Danica. More than that, he wanted her to come with him.

He smiled as the memory of her sitting on the couch, strumming his guitar while singing went through his mind. Her voice was so beautiful. It had been enough distance, he thought to himself, he was texting her. He texted that he had exciting news to tell her, and wondered if they could meet up.

Her heart leapt with his text. Luke had respected her need for distance, and she was grateful, but she had really missed him. She assumed that he had gotten help and thought that was the news that he had to tell her. She felt her own heart swell with excitement at a positive change.

Hope sang the notes without words in her heart all of that day. She asked Maria to watch Phoebe for her so that she could give Luke her undivided attention for something so monumental. That evening when they met Luke held her to him tightly, kissing her forehead he said, " I found a new job in Franklin Tennessee, it's the break I have been looking for. I accepted and would like for you and Phoebe to go with me."

Danica felt nauseous as she wiggled out of his embrace and looked at him while sitting down. She then proceeded to share his behavior with him from the last night that they had been together, hoping that he would see the seriousness of it all. He frowned, telling her that was all in the past.

" If it is not dealt with, it becomes our present and our future," Danica replied, the tears filling her eyes.

Luke was not ready to admit that he had a problem, making the present conversation very uncomfortable for him. He became angry at the thought that she may force him to get help. He had tried support groups as well as therapy, and none of them helped. He did love Danica though, and he wanted her to come with him, so he calmed his anger and said, "Being away from my parents will help."

"I need you to make more of a commitment to healing before I pack up and follow you with Phoebe," Danica replied.

Luke felt his anger flare up as he said, "Moving is a commitment to my healing, I cannot heal here."

Danica remembered her past life session, she remembered being Luece, leaving her ocean to follow him so many centuries before. She had not been able to tell him all that she had learned because he was always buzzed or drunk before she could share that information. At this moment in time she knew it would sound crazy if she told him any of it, especially with the heated emotions. As a therapist, she recognized repeating patterns. This was just a very extreme example.

Even though she loved Luke, she knew that if he did not get help she would be putting herself and Phoebe in a difficult if not dangerous situation. These are the moments, the choices, that shape our soul for lifetimes to come. They affect our children, our legacy, and as such should be weighed against the future of those that come after us, as Danica did when she brought her daughter into consideration as part of the decision.

Saying goodbye felt unbearable, but to put herself and especially Phoebe into danger, well, that was not an option. She remembered that moment, the words that came out of her mouth as gut wrenching emotional pain tore through her being. "I cannot go with you, take my daughter, uproot my practice, if you cannot commit to getting help. I will not put either one of us in that type of danger."

Luke looked at her, the pain evident on his face. "I know I have a problem, I am working on it in my own way. We have a connection, I know that you feel it. I love you."

She almost faltered in that moment as happy memories flooded her mind. Evening walks, new songs, his touch and the way that his skin felt against her finger tips. Phoebe was her saving grace. She may have, once again, followed him in the present life saying "come what may" to the consequences if it were only her, but she would not put Phoebe through that. "I can't," slipped out of her mouth.

She wiggled out of his embrace, as silent tears rolled down her face. The pain, such excruciating pain as if her soul was being ripped in half. She did not look up as she went out the door. She knew that she wasn't that strong. She would have seen the tears on his own face.

He left two weeks later, selling anything that he could not put in one U-Haul. He was excited about the opportunities that awaited him, but devastated over leaving Danica. He was hurt and angry that she could be so cold.

Danica took a week off of work, though she felt that a month would be more beneficial. The first day after Luke left she sat on the couch all day, processing as she called it. Maria had taken a few days off as well, "No one should sit alone in their darkness," she told Danica.

Danica remembered those years that she would have drank the pain away. She was grateful that she had found help, and Maria. Her friendship with Maria had brought so much good into her life.

During that week off Danica went for another past life session. She wanted to understand more of the connection that she was feeling, why it hurt so much. This time she went back to the beginning, the very beginning. " We are of the same breath," she told Maria.

"Ah, twin flames, they have a hard time together, often because of all the baggage they pick up throughout their lifetimes together. That explains why your connection is so deep though." Maria said.

So Luke started his new life in Tennessee while Danica sat by her ocean. They started new lives, each in their own ways. They both, though, felt the other as the years slipped by.

PART SIXTEEN

I could feel the storm, though I could not see ahead.

Perhaps if my eyes were open, but they were closed instead.

In fear I had them squeezed, as tight as they could go.

I didn't want to peek, I didn't want to know..

what was in front of me.

My boat tossed with the waves, my fingers tightly clutching the oars.

Not moving, barely breathing; where was the shore?

Then my internal whisper nudged me, as it echoed through my chest,

"Trust me, let me navigate, two hundred feet is always best.

Just two hundred feet in front of you, that's all you need to see,

Keep your fears silenced while you focus now on me,

and we will navigate a sea

with increments of two hundred feet."

A decade had passed since Danica had seen Luke. She was at the store picking something up for Phoebes high school dance when she bumped into Luke's mom. Her face lit up as she hugged Danica, asking how she had been.

She told Danica of Luke's marriage and then divorce and how well he was doing financially in Tennessee. Danica listened, mentally telling her heart to stop racing. She had thought about him through the years but had not seen his parents, even though they had loved her. She hugged Luanne once more before racing off to get Phoebe.

Danica had dated here and there throughout the years, but there had never been the connection that she had felt with Luke, and she wasn't willing to settle. She knew that she had made the right decision for herself and Phoebe, but through the years she had questioned it. Running into Luke's mom brought it to the surface again.

When she had been in school to become a therapist one of her professors had said something profound that had stuck with her. It would come to the surface of her thoughts, helping he navigate through difficult decisions without giving her power away. "You cannot ignore monsters away. Once you have turned on the light and have seen what is in the shadows, you cannot unsee it. You must learn to walk with your shadows while keeping on the light."

She had taken that to mean that we all walk with truths. Sometimes we chose to ignore them because they do not feel as good as the lie that we have been told or tell ourselves. In applying it to her situation with Luke the truth was she loved him, but alcoholism was the monster. even with the lights on, the shadow it cast would have snuffed out all of the light. She felt at peace with this answer inside of her and let the subject go.

That night Luke texted her, "My mother said it was so good to see you."

The universe has this magical ability to piece synchronistic moments together that change our lives in positive ways when we yield to the possibility that reality is an option. In Danica letting go, the universe could take over. As she read the text, she was unsure what to do. Should she open this can of worms after she had just made peace with herself again?

She was happy in her life. At times, she became lonely, but she was always happy. She had become an energy healer, adding to her therapy practice. In helping to heal others, she was in essence healing herself. She was very careful who she kept close to her, realizing that our energy has limits, we need to be aware of who and what we are putting that energy into in order to use it to it's best ability to better our own lives.

Danica wanted advice before she responded to Luke's text. She went to the universe first, using her runes as guidance. They spoke of flowing with the river of life without losing sight of yourself. She read on that she had to release fears as well as soul contracts. When she shared it with Maria later that day she said, "You will never know exactly where the river wants to take to you if you cling to the banks, afraid of all the possibilities."

Maria had her own conversation with the universe before she met with Danica. She had become like a daughter to her, and she wanted what was best for her in all of her lives. Maria had read of hope with healing, feeling that it was all too serendipitous to not be orchestrated by a higher power, no matter how she felt personally about Luke. So she encouraged Danica to reach out, but to keep herself awake and aware of what unfolded.

Danica's reply text opened up the lines of communication between herself and Luke again. He told her of his job, how he loved it, how healing that the move had been for him. The change had helped him overcome many of the negative habits that he had acquired through out his life.

His broken marriage had added to the determination to change those patterns. He still drank alcohol, but had learned moderation as he himself healed, using a combination of group therapy as well as a personal therapist. "I could not have healed at home. There were too many patterns that I had set in motion. In order to override them I had to reset my life. I would not have left had we not experienced what we did, but it was one of the most fearful times of my life. I realized through that experience that fear has it's place, but not as a guidance system. Fear walks with growth, especially when we start to stray from our negative, comfortable habits," he told Danica.

Danica agreed with him. She could see how throughout her life when change was necessary fear would hold her back, whispering to her that there was comfort in the old ways. She would have to give it a little "flick" of thought, as she called it, and fear would change to excitement.

Texting back and forth with Luke she felt fear raise it's head, nodding at her. What was she doing? Here she was encouraging Luke to take residence in her head and heart. The only explanation that she had was that it felt like the right thing to do.

She kept seeking her friends guidance, as well as guidance from her daily talk with the universe. She took it one text, one phone call at a time. Slowly her fear gave way to hope.

Luke's parents were having a wedding anniversary three months after Luke and Danica had started talking again. Luke was coming out to visit for it. He and Danica were both a little nervous about seeing each other again.

Danica thought back to the past life sessions that she had, remembering the longing she had felt in those centuries before for Luke.

Time is a funny thing like that, especially with cycles. Sometimes what was is, and what will be are already. When you look at the bigger picture, oftentimes time becomes irrelevant, though my wrinkles would beg to differ.

Danica went to the airport to get Luke, her stomach churning in anticipation of their meeting. Luke saw her as he got off of the escalator. Their eyes met and their faces lit up. And there was no time. No past or future, just that very present moment.

Danica smiled inside and out, grateful for their separate time of healing. That feeling of fear due to separation and trauma was gone, because they had now learned how to be one with themselves. That the universe led them together once again, well, tears of gratitude ran down Danica's cheeks as she rested her head on Luke's shoulder, hugging him. They were not young anymore, but neither were they old, Danica felt that they were just the right age to start a new adventure together.

The following days were a happy blur for Danica. She helped Luke's mom with decorations and finishing touches during the day, and spent her evenings with Luke. He would only be home a week, so they wanted to spend as much time together as they could. Danica was trying to live in each moment as she felt the moments were speeding up.

Luke's relationship with his parents had also healed through the years. John becoming softer as he aged. This added to the positivity of the week and their anniversary event.

As they picked up plastic cups and took down streamers after the event, Luke's heart was heavy. He loved Danica, he had missed so many things about her. She had finally shared all of her past life sessions with him. He accepted what she said, but had no memories himself beyond his present life. Some of his addictions had made portions of his present life blurry as well. He believed

Danica, especially with the connection that he felt. He was the happiest when he was near her.

He couldn't move back to Beaufort, though. There had been a few moments, a few memories, that made him want to revert to his old habits. He knew he wanted a future with Danica, but it could not be in Beaufort.

He felt that they had wasted enough time apart, so he was frank with his thoughts. He asked her about moving to Franklin with him, and then shared what he was experiencing by being back home. She answered that she wanted to be with him, but that was a huge decision that involved Phoebe, and she would have to think about it.

Danica got out the old recordings of her past life sessions. Being an energy healer as well as a therapist, part of what Danica helped others to overcome were their limiting patterns. She knew that she had a pattern with Luke. She felt that if she listened to her recordings, she could narrow that pattern down, hopefully breaking it.

One part of the recording resonated with her more than the others, Luece leaving her ocean and never coming back. It had cost her the gift of immortality. She had given her power away to Hades out of love, sacrificing herself. Bingo, Danica thought. She loved the ocean in this life as well. She could see that through out the lifetimes that they had, she had left what she loved to follow him because of love.

She had traveled all over, but the Atlantic sang the song that her heart knew all of the notes to. Franklin was in the land far away from her ocean. How could they both get what they wanted without sacrificing what they needed?

Danica got out her tools of divination, asking for guidance. As she calmed her mind a thought popped into it. "What about another coastal town?"

That made the most sense. It would be a big move for sure, and her business was full to overflowing. She could build that back up elsewhere as well, she felt. She had spoken with Phoebe, she was excited to move anywhere, so that had taken that fear. All of these thoughts raced through her head as she went to meet Luke.

She shared all of her thoughts with him, knowing that it would now be up to him as well. Now that she had seen the pattern, she would not repeat something that she now had the knowledge to change. He smiled and said, "I think that is a great idea! Lets look at some towns together."

That was the beginning of an extraordinary adventure together in this life. They moved to a beautiful city, Virginia Beach, Virginia and opened a practice together. From there they created a program to help families walk through addictions together, looking at it as a familial disease and healing it together.

Luke learned what Samiel and Hades did not, that power is elusive in many of its forms, but we each have this incredible power within ourselves to create with. We are so afraid of our own magnificence that like a game of hot potato we toss it to the closest person hoping to achieve peace if it is no longer our responsibility. Danica learned that she had her own link to the divine. She learned that she was whole of herself, but was able to appreciate the unity with others.

He and Danica had claimed their own power separately and then together. Now they were using it to change the lives of others around them as well as themselves. And here, my reader, since the title states a possible fairy tale I will add, they lived happily ever after.

Social Media

Etsy: @TimelessTales2Tell

YouTube: @timelesstalestotell

Instagram: @TimelessTellerofTales

Email: Esther@TimelessTalesToTell.com

About the Author

Esther Tucker is a registered nurse, holistic practitioner, teacher and co-creator of *The Oracle of Runes*. She began writing as a teenager and has published work in *Chicken Soup for the Soul*. *Hades and the Morning Star: a Possible Fairy Tale*, is her first eagerly awaited novel.